'I found this book soooo funny. I couldn't put the book down because it was so interesting and relatable ... I would 10000% recommend this to everyone and hope that there will be a sequel to the book!'

**Cleo, aged 15**

'Very funny. I couldn't put it down after I started reading it.'

**Aiko M, aged 12**

'Hilarious ... the book has the funniest moments I can really relate to.'

**Matthea, aged 14**

'This novel was hilarious and really captured the reality of school rather than everyone's normal expectations. I loved it!'

**Eliza B, aged 13**

'Hilarious, exciting and engaging, it grips you with its wit and relatability.'

**Jessica Y, aged 12**

'Believable characters and incredibly funny. I really enjoyed it.'

**Sienna R, aged 14**

'Extremely entertaining.'

**Amrita, aged 12**

'Brilliantly written – and it made me laugh out loud.'

**Fenella, aged 13**

'Not only is this book incredibly believable, but it is also hilarious.'

**Ciara M, aged 12**

'I couldn't recommend it more highly.'

**Daisy, aged 12**

'Hilariously funny and dripping with sarcasm.'

**Maya, aged 13**

—
... unique personality.'

**Poppy, aged 13**

'It was one of the best books I've ever read ... I never knew
what w...

..., aged 12

'India Smythe is guaranteed to make you laugh.'

**Anne, aged 11**

'Just as good as The Territory – my favourite book this year.'

**Sophie, aged 12**

'India Smythe is truly one of a kind.'

**Chelsea, aged 13**

'Brilliant, funny, immersive Bildungsroman about trust.'

**Violet, aged 12**

'It was an interesting and gripping read, the plot flowed so well.'

**Rose, aged 13**

'Laugh-out-loud portrayal of a rather quirky teenage girl.'

**Emma, Year 8**

'India Smythe isn't cool, she isn't perfect, but she's a hilarious and intriguing character.'

**Indy, aged 11**

'Witty and interesting. India Smythe made me appreciate my own life!'

**Hope, aged 14**

'Bubbly, vivacious and with ever growing confidence, India navigates her way through her love life and becomes a witty heroine.'

**Jessie, aged 14**

'I thought this book was lots of fun! I would recommend to all ages.'

**Grace, aged 12**

'Originally witty!'

**Lily W, aged 13**

'A witty and down to earth book.'

**Annalise H, Year 9**

for Noa, Alba and Ned

# India Smythe
# Stands Up

Sarah Govett

Marotte
www.marottebooks.com

First published in 2019
by Marotte Books Ltd
51 York Avenue, London SW14 7LQ

www.marottebooks.com
Text © Sarah Govett 2019

A CIP catalogue record of this book is available from the British Library.

Print ISBN 978-1-9161526-0-1

Typeset by Elaine Sharples
Printed and bound by PULSIO PRINT

Cover illustration by Nina Duckworth

Overall cover design by Anne Glenn

My name's India, India Smythe.

Pronounced Sm-I-I-I-I-I-I-the. Like you're stretching the 'I' between perfectly capped and whitened teeth and boasting at the same time.

Yes, it's an embarrassing name. Don't blame me – I didn't choose it.

I come from generation after generation of not massively high achieving but perfectly happy Smiths. Then, *BAM*, Grandad's born and he decides that our name's what's been holding our family back. Smith is not the name of success. Smith is too common. How about Smythe?

Honest to God. I've seen the birth certificate. Malcolm (that's Grandad) and Jill (Nan) Smith produced the first of the Smythes – Andrew Smythe – my Dad. You've got to give it to Grandad, I suppose. Dad is a pretty successful dentist, so maybe the I-I-I-I-I-I worked. But even so, if they were that desperate to posh up their family, couldn't they just have built a fountain on their driveway or joined a golf club or something instead of tacking up our surname for generations to come?

So, Smythe's bad enough, but India too! It's the sort of name that's cool on girls who actually have a bit of

Indian ancestry. But otherwise, there is no excuse for naming someone after a country. There aren't exactly loads of 'France's and 'Germany's out there, are there? So why is India acceptable? Apparently, Dad (during his pre-dentist 'in a band' phase) had gone out with loads of girls with normal names and Mum had refused to call me the name of any girl he'd got off with.

He hadn't got off with an India.

I have no idea why my parents thought it was OK to tell me this. It wasn't. Just thinking about Dad, the stud, pulling loads of randoms makes me feel horribly sick.

It's not that he's completely rough. Dad's got the same longish dark curly hair and greeny-brown eyes as me, but a bigger nose and smaller lips. A sort of low-rent Aidan Turner. (Come to think of it, that's probably why Mum fell for him. She loves a bit of *Poldark*.) And Amy Levens did actually flirt with Dad a bit at my last birthday. Genuinely. She did her whole neck-45-degrees-to-the-right, slightly-wider-eyes thing, which she thinks makes her look much older and really sexy, but actually makes her look like a half-strangled chicken.

Dad totally loved it though. He pretended to find it 'difficult to cope with' but he kept on bringing it up afterwards till Mum just exploded at him.

Mum's like one of those volcanoes in Sicily and places. She simmers away for ages – odd puff of smoke

– you're not quite sure if she's in a massively bad mood or not and then, suddenly – *BOOM* – there's molten lava everywhere and she's doing her best screaming banshee impression.

I should also point out that Dad's definitely not a paedo. Amy Levens has massive boobs and looks about twenty-one and it's not like Dad fancied her or was flirting with her AT ALL; it's just that he LOVED the fact that a teenage girl thought he was hot.

Mum was reading an article about 'watershed moments' this morning at breakfast. She's started Article Club with some local mum friends. It was originally going to be Book Club, but no one ever finished the books so they decided to lower the word count. Anyway, the article was going on about how your whole life's direction pivots on these tiny events, the significance of which you might not even get at the time, and for once I actually think it had a point. That's how school is anyway.

My first potential watershed moment came right at the start of Year 7. It was my first day at St Mary's School for Girls (heavy on the Saint) as a super-innocent eleven-year-old and they did this really lame quiz so you could 'get to know each other'. Meaning laugh at and then isolate and destroy the ones that didn't fit. We had to write the answers to three questions. The first two were stupid but fine:

- *Month you were born in*
- *Favourite colour.*

But Question 3 made my stomach double-triple-back-flip.

- *Name your favourite actor or actress.*

Aggghhhhhhh!!!! Disaster!!!!!!

Now for most people this wouldn't be a problem. But for me – it was. Massively so. Mum and Dad aren't so bad. They really love me and everything and are always telling me so. Embarrassingly frequently and often when other people can hear. But they've always been super strict about what I can watch. Want to protect my 'impressionable mind'.

Back when I was in Year 6 we were on holiday at this random kind of up-market caravan park place in Devon that had movie night at seven every evening. The first night there *Dirty Dancing* came on. Harmless classic, you might think. Raunch factor: 4.5/10. Oh no. Not for the Smythes. Dad leapt across the room to attach himself to the front of the screen, blocking the view of at least thirty eleven- to fifteen-year-olds. It was the bit, the only bit, where Baby took her top off. I might as well have been watching hardcore porn.

'India,' he squealed, finally peeling himself off the screen. 'You're not watching this filth. You're coming with me to play ping-pong. NOW.'

I had to spend the rest of the holiday in hiding, walking at least ten metres in front of or behind him, and trying out different hairstyles as a form of proto-disguise. It didn't work. There's not much point skulking behind a pool table with a French plait if someone then spots you and shouts out, 'Nobody puts Baby in the corner.'

So imagine how many actual recent films, films with guys in, that I got to watch. And forget about through my old primary school friends or on the Internet or anything. I went to a really sheltered primary school – a village one that combined classes for Years 1 and 2 as there were so few pupils, and that, thinking back on it now, might have been run by a cult. We had meditation instead of assembly and loads of the teachers played the guitar and wore gold-flecked, tasselled headbands. Mum chose the school when she was going through a bit of a release-her-inner-hippy stage. This was back when she called Dad 'Andy' and he called her 'Sam'. Then we moved to the Surrey suburbs and she shifted into a secure-good-grades-for-my-daughter-at-a-high-pressured-institution stage. Plus, this area's quite stuck-up so Dad's now Andrew (they even experimented with Drew for a week – terrible) and Mum's Samantha, as if adding a few syllables to your name helps you rise up an equivalent number of rungs on the social ladder.

*And* back then in Year 7 I didn't have a phone and even now I only have a museum-level Nokia 'just for emergencies' and 'so as not to stifle my imagination'. There's an article about Internet bullying and smartphones causing sleep disruption laminated and stuck to our fridge next to another one about how all the Silicon Valley billionaires don't let their children do anything other than crochet and stir mud with a stick.

'If it's good enough for them, it's good enough for you, India. They know what they're doing.' Where's the article about bullying and sleep deprivation from the stress of being twenty years out of date? At least my phone's so old it's mistaken for a style statement. I pretend that it is.

But my point is, that third question – *name your favourite actor or actress* – was one I was completely unequipped to answer. And it's scarred me so much that as soon as I think about it, that choice, time loops back on itself and I'm there in the classroom. Eleven years old again.

*I take a deep breath to calm my erratic breathing. Who to write? Who to write??????? Please don't let it be someone lame. Please let it be someone halfway acceptable.*

*'OK, time's up everyone,' smiles our well-meaning teacher-come-executioner, Ms White. My mind is a blank. A total blank. The only film I can think of is* Dirty Dancing. *With a shaking hand I scribble 'Patrick Swayze', fold my piece of paper in half and pass it to the front.*

*Ms White smiles again. Her teeth are a bit yellow. I hadn't noticed it at first. She should go to my dad.*

*'Here's the fun bit,' she trills. 'I'll pick out three pieces of paper and everyone gets to guess who wrote them!'*

*When she speaks, it's like every word she says has a built-in exclamation mark. What! A! Terrible! Idea!*

*'Remember there are no right or wrong answers!'*

*I pray that she's right, but every part of me knows that it's a lie. A big, fat lie.*

**Strike one:**

*'Month you were born in ... April.'*

*Friendly sniggers. I don't get it. Most people here have gone to the same primary school so there seem to be lots of things I don't get.*

*'Favourite colour ... yellow!'*

*Ms White sounds as excited as if she'd stumbled*

across the secret to wiping out superbugs. Or maybe it's just because the colour matches her teeth.

'Favourite actor or actress … Chris Helmsworth.'

Everyone cheers. My heart sinks. There clearly is a right answer. Chris Helmsworth is the right answer. A slim, alabaster arm with absolutely no bobbles from in-growing hairs shoots up; its trajectory fans away perfectly washed blond hair.

'Yes, Lisa?'

'April Jones,' comes the guess.

The paper is turned over to reveal April's name. Affectionate arm-squeezes, high-fives all round. April and Lisa are popular. The social elite. I may have only been at this school for a couple of hours, but some things take less than ten minutes to figure out.

Back to the lion's den.


**Strike two**:

'November' … 'pink' … 'Chris Helmsworth' … 'That's right, it's Nicole Hughes.'

Oh God, help me now. I have just committed accidental social suicide. Please don't pick my one. Please, please, please.

God clearly doesn't appreciate years of irregular church attendance followed by last minute desperate begging.

***Strike three:***

*'August.' Oh bollocks.*

*'Green.' Bollocks bollocks.*

*'Patrick Swayze.' Bollocks to infinity.*

*A tidal wave of jeering laughter sweeps the room.*

*'Is he even still alive?'*

*'He must be like a hundred now.'*

*'Who?'*

*Apparently* Dirty Dancing *is no longer the hit it once was.*

*Search beam eyes sweep the room to identify the loser who wrote this.*

*'Guesses anyone?' Ms White, all perma-smile. Like the corners of her mouth are Superglued to her cheekbones.*

*Names are suggested and it's really obvious even to a newcomer like me that these are not the cool kids. If school popularity rankings were a cross section through an ocean, with the popular kids being the flying fish leaping around the waves on top, these were the names of the fish in the Midnight Zone – swimming about in the cold and dark with weird torch-like things hanging off their foreheads.*

*And, what's even worse, even these kids look offended when their names are shouted out. Like they'd ever write Patrick Swayze?!*

*Ms White takes control again, the smile still championing her face.*

*'OK, let's find out who wrote this then!'*

*She turns over the paper. Goodbye love. Goodbye happiness. Hello head torch.*

*And then, somehow, the axe doesn't fall. Ms White looks puzzled, clearly an emotion she's unfamiliar with. Her facial muscles are spasming, struggling out of perma-smile mode.*

*'Oh … that's strange. It looks like the person forgot to write their name on the paper… Oh well. Who wrote this then? Anyone?'*

*Silence.*

*In my panic I must have forgotten to write my name. Thank you panic! Thank you so much! I fix my eyes on a worn spot on the floor. It's the shape of France on a map. Well, France if it had invaded and nabbed a bit of northern Spain.*

*I'm pretty sure no one knows my handwriting yet.*

*I am going to survive this.*

The Fence.

Harmless boundary dividing two different plots of land? No. That's not it at all. Not when the plots in question are St Mary's Girls and St Joseph's Boys. And not when the boundary is a hundred and fifty metres of two-metre-high wire diamonds through which you are highly visible on both sides. Especially not when it is THE ONLY place during school time where you can talk to boys and where your mere presence and exactly who you talk to will be dissected more thoroughly than a formaldehyded frog.

We did dissection this morning in Biology. Of a pig's eyeball. It was so grim. You cut across the centre of the eye with a scalpel and the vitreous humour, basically thick black jelly, seeps out and I nearly puked. I've always had a thing about eyes and now I know I'll never smell another rose in case I accidentally burst my eyeball on a thorn in the process.

I make a point of NEVER going to the Fence. That is a bit loserish in itself but far less loserish than being spotted talking to the wrong person from St Joseph's. I don't know enough of the right guys to ensure that this isn't going to happen. There is also always the relatively high chance that you'll get stopped by Mrs Millican, the R.S. teacher who has a nose ring and thinks she's young and cool and wants to talk about 'personal issues'. Not that anyone talks to her any more. Not since Lauren Melrose confided in her about being adopted and Mrs Millican told just about everyone. And the award for most awesome pastoral care goes to...

Now people just make up stuff to tell her. Like when last week April Jones 'confided' that she'd kissed her brother and really enjoyed it just to see how Mrs Millican would react. It made me almost like April for a split millisecond. Almost.

Anyway, today was freakishly windy. The sort of day when all the teachers start talking about weird weather patterns and global warming until it's nice and sunny again and they forget all about it, like a form of dementia. It was the end of first break and I was walking along the path to the English block, clutching my overdue English homework in one hand and trying to calm my bouffanting hair with the other. A one-hundred-metre walk was taking me forty years back to the eighties. The homework was a poem on Loss. I was pretty proud of it. I'd used sibilance and assonance and made sure it didn't rhyme. A rhyming poem never got you more than a C. Or rather a 4. The whole school's now switched to the new 1-9 marking instead of A, B, C, D. Stop press! We had a whole assembly about it. The stupid thing is it hasn't really caught on at all. Last week, Meena got a 6 for her creative writing and was all like,

'Is that good?' and then Mrs Travers said, 'It's basically a B+,' and then everyone was happy.

So, I was walking along the path when this massive gust of wind, well … gusted, and my poem got blown out my hand and off towards the Fence. And not just some random, empty bit of Fence, but right up to where April and Lisa were standing, talking to two guys from St Joseph's. I didn't want to approach, to be anywhere near them. Lisa is all pale skin and blonde hair; April's got dark skin, cropped tight black curls and lips from a Revlon advert. Neither has had a single spot in all my time at St Mary's. It's never good to stand next to perfection. Especially when perfection is a complete bitch.

But there was nothing for it. I had to catch my poem or get a Friday afternoon detention. I half walked, half ran to the Fence. I really should have just committed to one or the other. What I was doing, essentially a speed-walk, is probably the least cool method of movement possible. The Mr Bean of motion. As I drew closer, I saw that the guys in question were Anthony and Ennis. I'd never talked to them but knew them by sight. Everyone did. They were THE GUYS in our year to talk to. The male Aprils and Lisas of this world. Up close though they were actually slightly unimpressive. Ennis was fit but short. I bet I'd be properly taller if I wore any of my normal heels. And Anthony had a few bits of acne. Not the biggest outbreak ever but still enough to reach-for-the-Clearasil-and-stay-off-school-till-it's-gone level. But I admit they gave off a kind of 'I'm attractive because I'm SO CONFIDENT' vibe. And I guess if you're called Ennis but are cool despite it and aren't the victim of loads of penis related jokes maybe you are really something after all?

I mumbled a lame sort of, 'Hi,' and tried to look as relaxed and pretty (or least awful) as I could. I look reasonably symmetrical from front on, but my left profile is significantly better than my right, so I adjusted position accordingly and thanked God that I hadn't taken out my contact lenses at the start of break, even though the left one definitely had a small hair in it and was scratching my eye. What's a bit of cornea damage compared to a damaged reputation?

'Nice hair, India,' Lisa laughed. Lisa only laughs with her mouth and never with her eyes. Partly because she is evil and has no soul. Partly because she has nice, white, evenly spaced teeth. And partly because she doesn't want to start Botoxing until her mid-twenties. Her words not mine.

'Hi,' I mumbled in reply, trying to bend down to retrieve my poem without flashing everyone. My skirt is admittedly a bit too short at the moment. It's really difficult to get it right, though. You obviously can't wear it knee-length, the way it comes, as that's tragic. Most people cut off the bottom and re-hem. There was no way Mum was going to let me do that. I once just made some sort of hint in that direction and you could see the lava start to bubble. I'm therefore stuck with the third, rubbish option of rolling up the waistband. One roll still isn't enough, though, so I'm a double-roll girl. But that does result in a pretty short skirt. And the appearance of a bit of a fat waist.

Then the wind (or karma punishing me for killing the massive spider in the bathroom this morning when I could have just trapped it with a glass and put it outside) picked up my poem again and chucked it over the fence.

Without thinking, I swore loudly. And I mean really swore. And then Anthony and Ennis didn't leap up to try and catch it or chase it down for me or anything and I thought, 'What idiots.' But then they started laughing and they asked my name. Anthony and Ennis asked for MY NAME!!!!!!!

'India, India Smythe,' I stumbled. I said my surname. I don't know why I said my surname. They didn't ask for my surname.

'Smythe?'

'It's Scottish.' I've started saying that. 'Smythe' does sound a bit Scottish and that seems to make people accept it and forget how horrific it is.

'Good to meet you, India Smythe,' Ennis grinned.

'Anthony's having a party on Saturday. Come. Bring a friend.' It was an instruction not an invitation, but I didn't care. I'd been asked to a party by one of the coolest guys at St Joseph's. And he did have amazing eyes. Spanish style with super-long lashes. Like a Franco brother. Movie star rather than fascist dictator. Maybe I could wear flats and then stand next to him all night without dwarfing him? Who cared about a lost poem or a detention? This lunch break had been a triumph!

Then the bell rang and, reluctantly, I turned to head to class, walking alongside April and Lisa and feeling pretty damn good actually. Like I'd met the Devil and survived. Like the Devil might actually like me a bit. Meena, about to enter the English block, turned and saw me and literally nearly fainted with surprise. I grinned stupidly at her to show I wasn't the victim of some weird body-swap and that all would be revealed later. I walked on another few metres when I heard this voice:

'Wait, wait!'

I turned to see another figure at the Fence. It wasn't Anthony or Ennis. It was a guy I'd never seen before. He had big, curly hair like me, but his had been blown right up by the wind, so it looked like his forehead went on and on forever. He had blue, puppy dog eyes and weirdly red cheeks. Strapped to his back was a cello case. He was not cool. In his outstretched hand he clutched my rescued poem. I ran back to the Fence where, without speaking, he rolled the poem into a tube and pushed it through the wire to me.

'Thanks,' I breathed. 'Thanks so much!'

'I'm Rich. Rich Evans,' he said – apparently another compulsive surname provider – and this smile broke out on his face. He had really deep dimples. You could probably fit a pea in one and I'm not even talking about a petit pois.

'I'm India. India Smythe,' I replied. He nodded and I didn't feel the need to mention the Scottish bit.

I ran back to the path and Lisa asked what *that* was. Like he didn't even deserve a who.

'No one. Just some loser.' The words instantly tasted sour in my mouth – like biting into a jelly bean that you think is watermelon but turns out to be cinnamon – and I felt really guilty. I mean this guy had just helped me and he seemed really sweet and here I was putting him down. All to get the approval of the two meanest girls in the year.

As I walked the last few steps to English I felt all these eyes on me. Girls, staring. At first I assumed they'd overheard me calling Rich a loser and were rightly judging me. But then I realised it was something else. It wasn't judgment, it was jealousy. They were jealous because I was suddenly in with April and Lisa.

And I started wondering whether this would be the second watershed moment of my life.

Authority's a spectrum.

At one end you have your Gillian Thomases, where everything they do is embarrassing and terrible. I can't believe I was ever friends with Gillian. Well, I can. It was the start of Year 7, I hadn't got to know Meena and Anna yet and I was desperate to attach myself to someone, anyone. Gillian sort of claimed me. We bonded over being the only two people at school without a smartphone. And her monobrow and sports obsession were less pronounced then.

At the other end, you have your April Joneses and Lisa Hartleys, and everything they do is respected and rated and people queue up to jump off a cliff after them.

Take last weekend. April had a Scrabble party. Not Gillian, April. Yes, I'm not kidding. I obviously wasn't invited, not being top strata cool and this being four days before the whole Fence triumph, but I have it on good authority (Amy Levens, who knows EVERYTHING) that Lisa, Anthony and Ennis went round to April's and played Scrabble. Played it ironically. Which somehow makes it cool. *Hey, we're like playing Scrabble. Aren't we hilarious as we're obviously far too cool to actually seriously be playing Scrabble, but we're still, like, playing.* And I bet they all enjoyed it in a smug ironic way.

I hate them. They're so scared of actually admitting to genuinely liking something that they're always hiding behind this shield of irony. Amy said it was all over Insta, which obviously I didn't see as my rubbish phone predates anything resembling apps and there's no way I'm looking at anything on our 'family shared computer' in the hall. *A shared space is a safe space. Aggghhhh!*

The same spectrum exists for teachers, and Mrs Higgins, our French teacher, is firmly placed at Gillian's end. We're supposed to call her Madame Higgins, which seems ridiculous as she has one of the worst French accents I've ever heard. Which part of France are you from? *Arrrrrhhh 'Arrogate-upon-Paris.* She also has so little authority that I actually feel really sorry for her.

As it's Thursday we had her for third period, straight after English, in one of the temporary classrooms at the bottom of the playing field. She wouldn't quite meet our eyes as she took the register. Lisa's in my French set and Mrs Higgins is terrified of her. Which is a terrible response as Lisa can smell fear. Mrs Higgins rarely asks Lisa a question and, if she does, Lisa makes a point of not answering and then there's this really awkward moment when Mrs Higgins is clearly deciding whether to demand an answer or pretend that she never asked the question in the first place. In the end she always cops out and chooses option two.

'Oh, where was I? Oo lah lah. Something about holidays. Les vacances. Je suis allée à Yorkshire.'

Today, though, Mrs Higgins made a crucial error. She left the room to get some photocopies she'd left in the staffroom and returned to find that Lisa had locked the door.

There is something really disturbing about watching a teacher beg. I mean they're supposed to have the power. But there was *Madame* Higgins, face pressed against the window, attempting angry face then disappointed face, but somehow just looking different shades of pathetic.

At last, she just totally surrendered all dignity and there came this terrible, almost moan of, 'Please, please let me in.' Part of me wanted to just march up and open the door and end the suffering. But more of me wanted to not be the friendless loser who let the teacher in. Particularly when Lisa and April were just starting to look at me like I might not be some four-day-old gum stuck on the bottom of their shoe. Opening the door would be tearing up my invitation to Anthony's party. I would be a bottom feeder forever. So I just sat there. Willing the end of lesson bell to toll.

Just before it did, Lisa slowly stood up and prowled to the door, flipping the lock open with her right hand.

'Madame Higgins, you must have accidentally locked yourself out,' she purred, the picture of innocence.

'I um … yes … oui … that must have been it. Zut alors!'

BRIIIIIINNNNNGGGGGG.

'Alors. Everyone take a worksheet on your way out and we'll look at them next lesson.'

Mrs Higgins put the pile of photocopies down on the desk and then sat, head lowered, blinking away tears.

I must never, ever get on the wrong side of Lisa Hartley.

So, Anthony's party is still happening and I'm still invited. April gave me the details at first break today as it's almost like her joint party as she's Anthony's girlfriend. She didn't seem totally happy about telling me, but she's definitely been nicer to me since the whole Fence thing. No one even laughed at me when I answered three questions in Physics today and that's April's doing. She definitely controls all laughter of the mocking variety in our school. Like there's a button she alone can push.

Now, the important bit – who to bring? Meena's the obvious choice, naturally. She's been my best friend at St Mary's since the middle of the first term. I think the moment we bonded was our first winter PE lesson. We were both drowning in the far too massive tracksuits that our mums had independently bought us with the idea that we'd maybe 'grow into them'. By the age of eighteen. Why buy more than one when you can make your emotionally vulnerable daughter look obese for her whole teenage life? I mean extra large – come on!!

I don't know why Mum would even think I'd ever grow into it. She's not even big herself. I mean she's got wide hips and doesn't look as good as she did in her twenties (which is why all photos of her up in the house are of her in her twenties), but she's in no way extra large. And all the women on Dad's side of the family are like these fragile bird skeletons (with beaks to match). So genetically I should be OK (but potentially big-nosed) as long as I don't permanently stuff my face.

Meena's also really ace. Not rated at St Mary's, I guess. She's too opinionated and clever for that. Meena's more like cool in the sense of a really loyal, really kind, funny friend. However, the three downsides to bringing Meena are:

1    Her parents are even stricter than mine (they're saving her for some nice Sikh boy) so we'd have to pretend that she's just coming over for a movie and sleepover night and hope that my mum doesn't talk to her mum.

2    Occasionally she rebels against this massive strictness by dressing … how can I put this…? A little bit slutty. Too much make-up and too much cleavage. But maybe that's just jealousy speaking. The rubbish thing, well one of the many rubbish things, about being young in the year is that you get boobs later than ANYONE else. I'm still waiting for something more than an A to appear. Bra sizes are like the opposite of exam grades. Before they invented numbered marking.

3    Meena has a 'thing' about Lisa. They used to be friends in primary school, but then Lisa binned her when they started St Mary's and Meena has never totally gotten over the rejection. She tends to act slightly crazy in Lisa's presence and has a weird obsession with Lisa's life, in particular her family's annual Christmas Party that she always used to be invited to.

But if I don't ask Meena, who else could I invite? The only other real option is Anna. Who's also lovely, but the reverse Meena: relaxed parents, no weird history with Lisa, but could benefit from a few more low-cut tops. Anna's always out in 'practical' clothes, typically bought at Gap or Mountain Warehouse. A polo neck when it's cold in winter, a fleece when it's windy, a cagoule when it rains. I don't know why this is so wrong, but it just is. I guess you're not supposed to be that well suited to your environment unless you're Bear Grylls or someone and I'm sure even he owns some normal clothes for weekends. She's also a member of the orchestra. Big minus sign. She says this is great as the orchestra is the one thing that's done jointly between St Mary's and St Joseph's so she meets loads of boys. She hasn't quite worked out yet that orchestra geeks don't count.

I don't think Anna's ever had a boyfriend. I mean, to be honest, I haven't really either. Not a proper one. I've snogged guys at parties and been on a few dates, but they've always been really awkward and I've always sort of frozen up or found the guy really boring. I seem to be attracted to really hot guys who invariably turn out to be really stupid.

There was this one guy, Yan. A friend of a friend of Anna's brother. Yan the beautiful. Yan the tall. Yan with cheekbones that could cut granite. But then he turned out to also be Yan the guy who's idea of a date is to go to the Green after dark and drink cider and then tell a really long, terrible story about breaking into a building site and 'taking a dump on the stairs'. He rolled around almost swallowing his tongue at his own hilariousness and then seemed stunned and mad that I didn't want to 'lie down' with him behind the benches.

Back to the matter in hand – there's no debate really. I'll have to ask Meena. God, I hope she can make it. There's no way I can go alone. And I really want to go!

Party night.

I couldn't eat all day as my stomach had shrunk to the size of a small orange – a Clementine or particularly dehydrated Satsuma perhaps – in anticipation. Mum didn't comment on it, my lack of appetite that is. Probably because even she admitted that the lunchtime quinoa and black bean bake she produced 'wasn't one of her best'. She only managed about three mouthfuls herself. Dad choked on his first bite and then made himself an omelette.

I changed about five times and ended up back in what I first put on. Tight, black, fake patent leather skirt, loose-ish top that's supposed to be 'caramel' but in my bedroom mirror looked a tiny bit beige (the least sexy colour of all time), 'natural tan' tights and gold flats. The tights were stupidly the hardest choice. It was a warm evening for November and I knew no one else would have tights on. They'd just have their beautifully tanned, smooth, long legs out in open-toe heels. Tights are for old people. Tights are a badge of shame. But it's better to be slightly shamed than to get out too white legs that even if just shaved might have a trace of stubble or a weird in-growing hair. Meena told me that I should get this make-up for legs instead. It's like a sort of foundation that you smear over your legs so it looks like you're borrowing someone else's skin. I should never listen to Meena. Luckily I tried some of this at home last week. It looked amazing and to start with I was all, 'Yay – miracle product – praise the name of Meena Chandra,' but then it turned out that if you sweat, even the tiniest bit, the foundation comes off your legs onto whatever you're sitting on. Mum made me scrub the sofa with this carpet shampoo at least five times. Whisk the shampoo, layer it on, leave for ten minutes, vacuum and repeat. Imagine if I hadn't trialled it? Imagine if I had shed my brown fake skin on Anthony's sofa like some sort of freakish snake? I'd have to insist on being homeschooled till I was eighteen.

The other difficult decision was what bra to wear. I don't mean like which of my array of beautiful lacy numbers. I don't have any. Mum wouldn't buy me any. Not that I've asked. It would be mortifying. She'd want to have 'that chat'. 'Woman to woman.' No, what I'm talking about is whether it was better to wear the plain black non-padded one or my one padded one. Meena bought the padded one for me for my last birthday. *Ultimate Lift*. My boobs look halfway decent in it. As long as you're not doing anything other than looking. If someone was to say, grab a feel, they'd be left clutching a handful of stuffing and it would be pretty obvious that there was little else going on. They might as well cup a pillow. So is the appearance of good stuff, followed by huge disappointment better or worse than upfront flat-chestedness? It was a difficult call. In the end I went for upfront non-padded combined with loose top that looks like it could be skimming curves (even though there aren't any).

The bell rang at seven on the dot and I raced downstairs to open it. Meena was standing on the doorstep in jeans and a jumper and very neutral make-up. That's what she always turns up in so her mum thinks she looks respectable. The question was – what was she wearing underneath?

The door shut and she whipped the jumper off. Any

worries I had evaporated as fast as a slushie in the Sahara. She looked amazing. Tightish, dark red halterneck top but not spilling out or anything. Not a trace of slutty. I take it all back. I'm a bad friend. There was no one in the whole world I'd rather go to Anthony's party with. Meena was awesome.

I grabbed my bag, keys and phone, opening the door ready to go out when Meena bundled me straight back into the house again.

'Aren't you forgetting something?'

I didn't get it.

'We've got to put on our make-up!' She looked at me like I was a complete moron even though it was her who was the denser in this instance. I could tell she already had some on and I'd already done my face too. Foundation, concealer, mascara, the whole shebang. I'd gone for 'natural' with pinkish lips and smokey eyes. Smokey-ish. Eyes that maybe vaped occasionally.

Apparently I knew nothing.

'The only thing that matters at parties,' Meena explained, 'is how you look in the photos that everyone's posting. No one remembers the actual party. But the photos will haunt you forever. Your attractiveness will be judged on them forever.'

She did an exaggerated sigh to emphasise how exhausting it was, explaining all this to such a simpleton.

'You don't understand, India, 'cos you don't have a smartphone.'

Everything always came back to this: my lack of proper phone. I felt like a caveman whose friends all had wheels and were wheeling all their stuff around everywhere really fast while he didn't; while he just had a square shaped lump of rock.

'And to look good in photos, India,' Meena continued, oblivious to the very realistic caveman tableau playing out in my brain, 'you have to wear *slightly* more make-up than normal. Contouring is key.'

I sent up a prayer of thanks that, even if my parents are set on turning me into a proto-Mormon, I at least have a friend who knows what's going on. I meekly followed Meena upstairs. We were going to take over the bathroom as that's the only place in the house with decent lighting. It's got spotlights plus fake candle bulbs on either side of the mirror so Dad can 'shave properly' a.k.a. spot and remove weird, randomly long eyebrow and ear hairs. I've seen him there, eyes watering, attacking himself with a pair of tweezers when he thinks no one can see. I tried the handle but it was locked.

'I'm having a bath, love,' Mum called. Short 'a'. As in rhymes with Cath. Mum just used a SHORT 'A' SOUND!!!

'A baaaarrrrrrth,' she repeated, flustered. 'BAARRRRTH.'

Mum's originally from Leicester and for some reason seems to think this is terribly shameful and tries to eradicate any trace of it from her accent. Short 'a' sounds to the firing squad. A chance survivor making it through was a sure sign she was knackered. She'll be mad about this now. Mad for a while.

The stupid thing is what Mum's totally failed to realise in her desperation to sound southern is that no one cares about short 'a's. People like them in fact. Regional accents are cool. Regional accents make you seem authentic and seem to massively up your chances of getting on TV. Far, far worse a crime is to overdo the fake southernness, to misuse the long 'a' – and this is something which she does, unashamedly, on a semi-regular basis. She's the only person I know who says PLAHstic when everyone knows it's plastic. Even Rosie Trevelyan's dad, who is the poshest person I've ever seen in real life, says plastic. ELAHstic is another classic. Plus Mum says 'fantastic' normally so there's absolutely no logic to it whatsoever.

Anyway, we abandoned the bathroom and instead bundled into my room. I sat on my bed while Meena attacked my face with a highlighter pen in time with a YouTube tutorial on 'maximising, minimising and defining'.

'I thought you said you knew how to do this?' I asked, losing confidence with every minute that ticked by and every brushstroke that required a cotton bud softened with E45 cream correction.

'I do. Well, CatrinX2000 does, and that's basically the same thing.'

It was definitely not basically the same thing.

After she'd 'given me some cheekbones', Meena darkened my brows and 'intensified' my lips. Then it was my turn to operate on her. She wouldn't let me look in the mirror until we were both finished. I think I was the better make-up artist. I only used eight cotton buds to her twelve.

When I was done, I popped my head out my bedroom and saw that the bathroom door was now open. Time to check on our handiwork. We tumbled inside and I flipped on the light switch, marched Meena towards the mirror and then full on gasped. A sort of strangled *I can't breathe and there's nothing Heimlich or anyone else can do to help me*. And this time it wasn't because I'd seen Mum's bottle of Femfresh at the side of the shower. It was us. It was all us. A close-up, well-lit horror show. Red blusher like war paint, eyebrows like a pair of slugs and eyes, eyes like Janice Tanner had gone all psycho again and had socked me one in the teacher no-go zone behind the Physics block. It wasn't quite as bad on Meena. Her darker skin tone somehow muted the effect slightly. I, however, looked like a freaky-ass doll from a Stephen King-esque horror. The producers of IT 2 would be ecstatic. *Forget the clown – we've found something much, much better.* I almost expected some scary music box plinky plonky slow-motion music to start up.

I ran back to my room with Meena at my heels yelping, 'Wait, wait.'

Tears were forming at the corners of my eyes but Meena hissed at me not to cry as I'd make my mascara run and she didn't want me to go all Alice Cooper over 'her creation'.

'Just stand still for a minute, put your head on one side. No the other side. Your good side. Now smile.' I forced the tears back in. I made my lips turn up at the corners. Meena took a photo on her phone and showed it to me. I pushed the screen away at first but she forced me to look. Slowly, ever so slowly I took it in. I … looked … great! Really, really great! Industrial Revolution-level smoky eyes, full dark lips and cheekbones. Cheekbones that would have made Yan turn green.

Meena, we adore you. Lay our lives before you.

'See?' she said, smugly.

I nodded, full of respect. 'Thanks, Meena.'

'It's very important we make a good impression tonight,' Meena continued. 'Lisa's obviously going to be there and if we get into the in-crowd we might be invited to her Christmas Party. She has an ice sculpture – did I tell you that? And profiteroles. *Trays* of them.'

I rolled my eyes. She'd told me this literally a hundred times. On and on about Lisa's stupid Christmas Party. But I couldn't get mad at her tonight after she'd done me this massive favour. Just imagine if I didn't have Meena for a friend? I wouldn't have known what to do at all! I would have looked like a total idiot at the party and absolutely minging in all the photos. Best. Friend. Ever.

We managed to get out the house without a proper goodbye to my mum and dad, who were both already sitting down for dinner. I thought it was better this way. Dad's face is a bit like universal indicator in Chemistry – changing colour to a kind of mottled purple if he as much as glimpses me in lip gloss – and I didn't think he'd be totally on board with the whole 'make-up looks better on photos' thing.

'Do you have a bag with you?' Mum called out as she heard the front door open. Mum's obsessed with being prepared and carries loads of supplies everywhere. In her world, an emergency clothes change/snack/umbrella/reading-and-note-taking-opportunity lies round every corner. 'There's plenty of plAHstic bags in the kitchen cupboard if you need one.'

'I'm fine,' I shouted back as Meena sniggered next to me.

'I'll pick you up at ten,' Dad yelled.

'Midnight!' I countered, indignantly. This was a proper party. Lots of people probably wouldn't even turn up until ten.

'Ten-thirty!'

I rolled my eyes, but knew from Dad's high-pitched squeal that this was as good as it was going to get. The higher he goes up the octaves, the less likely he is to back down. This morning I'd suggested that we took the night bus back from the party. Said that it wasn't a big deal. That lots of my friends did it. Dad shot from baritone to soprano in a millisecond. The conversation went a bit like this:

Dad:   India [big sigh] *India* – do you know what sort of people take night buses?

Me:    Teenagers coming back from parties?

Dad:  No. God, India, sometimes you're so naïve.
      Samantha, tell her she's being naïve.

Mum:  India, you're being naïve.

Dad:  Paedophiles take night buses. Rapists take night
      buses. Hookers take night buses.

Mum:  Paedophiles, rapists and hookers.

Dad:  Probably terrorists too.

Mum:  Probably.

There was no point. The discussion was going absolutely nowhere and I knew that if I kept on pushing it, me and Meena wouldn't even be allowed to take the bus TO the party. At least I managed to make Dad agree to wait in the car round the corner when he picked us up. The deal was that he wasn't allowed anywhere near the house. Wasn't to approach the front door.

'Imagine the front path is landmined,' I told him. 'And you're not that guy you like in *The Hurt Locker*.'

Me and Meena got a few strange looks as we got on the bus and I almost wanted to turn round and go straight back home again. I swear one girl actually sniggered. Sniggered at my face.

'They're just jealous,' Meena whispered into my ear. 'All their men are looking at us, so they're jealous.'

I nodded. The sniggering girl didn't look typically jealous and didn't even have a man with her, but maybe she was sat there, picturing her man and imagining him wanting me instead. Yes, that might be it. Oh God, I hope that's it.

We got off the bus a stop early, as it was only seven forty-five and April had said eight. As we stepped onto the pavement, it struck me that I didn't know if eight actually meant eight? Was punctuality now ironically cool? Surely not. But then I'd have said that about Scrabble and been massively wrong. *Zoella says timeliness and board games are so in this season.* Or did 'eight' mean don't arrive before eight-thirty unless you're a complete loser? Another totally viable alternative. Aggghhhhh!! This was the trouble with suddenly leap-frogging up the social strata. You didn't know the rules. You could be caught out at any time. If Anna said, 'Come round for a pizza at seven,' there weren't any issues. Hell, I could turn up at six-thirty to help pick the toppings and no one would raise an eyebrow. All my social life so far had totally failed to prepare me for moments like this.

We ended up deciding on eight-fifteen, which gave us about half an hour to kill. We had to stop loitering around the bus stop though as buses kept on stopping, thinking we wanted to get on and then the drivers shot us massive evils as we waved them away.

We super slow walked up the main road and then

down the second street on the right until we reached our destination: 22 Acacia Drive. Not an Acacia in sight. Instead, a stylish tiled front path, classy hanging porch light, bay tree in a pot and loud music pulsing out the door and windows. This was it. For the first time in my life, I was where it was at. Where anyone who was anyone wanted to be. I had imagined this moment so many times.

In my imagination, I hadn't felt slightly sick.

'Can we go round the block again?' I asked Meena in a small voice.

'Sure,' Meena agreed a bit too readily, sounding about six too. A horrible, creeping awareness that all Meena's knowledge about parties and what to do and what to wear was probably just taken from American TV shows and dodgy YouTube channels rather than real life began to dawn. She was allowed out less than me. So how could she know??? I was such an idiot.

'And you're sure about this make-up?' I whispered, my voice wavering. 'Sure that this is what everyone does?'

'I'm sure,' Meena replied. But she didn't sound as sure as she had in my room. She sounded a hell of a lot less sure now. 'I mean, they wear tonnes of make-up on *Riverdale*.'

OH. NO. NO. NOOOOOOOOO!!!!!!!!!!!!!!!!!!!

We did a lap of the block. Then another. Then another. It was now nine. We had to get it together. We had to go to this party. We couldn't blow off Anthony from St Joseph's party. That would be actual, irreversible, social suicide.

We were back outside 22 Acacia Drive. I forced my legs up the path. Left, right, left, right, left, right and stared at the doorbell. I don't think President Kennedy was as freaked out by the idea of pressing the red button and starting global nuclear war when Krushchev got that little bit too close to Cuba.

'You ring it,' I hissed.

Meena was more confident than me. She normally took the lead in things like this, but this time she point-blank refused.

'I'm the plus one,' she said, shaking her head incredulously as if I'd just suggested she move to Siberia and start a logging business. 'The plus one *never* rings the bell.'

'OK.'

Then I paused. Just completely froze. 'Can we walk round the block one more time?'

'OK.'

We were about to turn when, without warning, the door opened. It was Lisa. Lisa framed in the doorway, a bottle of beer dangling from her hand like a prop in a fashion shoot. Lisa looking incredible in knitted wool hot pants and a T-shirt that said 'bookworm'. Her legs were totally bare yet flawless. (How was she not freezing?!!!!! Maybe scientists have discovered that 90% of body heat is lost through the buttocks. So as long as they're covered – you're fine.) Lisa with virtually no make-up on. Hair down. Fresh faced, dewy, perfect. No. NO NO NO!

'India?'

Lisa started laughing. Openly laughing. At us.

'I thought I heard someone.'

I didn't say anything. I opened my mouth and no sound came out.

Another figure appeared next to Lisa. April. Also from a different season. Wearing what looked like a man's denim shirt and flip-flops, which seemed to make her legs look even longer than normal. And subtle make-up. Really subtle make-up. A touch of dark pink on her bee-stung lips and that was basically it.

'What took you so long? Were you … making yourself look pretty?!' A cackle erupted from April's perfect mouth and I hated her. I hated her almost as much as I hated Meena and CatrinX2000 at that moment.

'COME IN!' a shout from behind and a very drunk Anthony pushed his way through the people lining the hall, and dragged us into the house.

'This is my party so it's my job to welcome the guests!'

'You're such a gentleman,' April purred, stroking his arm territorially.

Anthony didn't respond. His gaze had clouded over and he looked at me, confused.

'And who are you? I didn't order a hooker. Did anyone order me a hooker?'

'I'm … er … India, India Smythe… You invited me… By the Fence.' The confusion was still there in his eyes and apparently I could now only speak in fragments. Anthony didn't know who I was. I'd made so little impression on him that he didn't know who I was and … here's the crowning glory … thought I was A HOOKER. The next moment he'd be putting me on a night bus. This was a disaster. A disaster that trumped all disasters ever. There was only one thing I was sure about – if my name was getting trashed, if I was going down, I was taking Meena down with me.

'And this is my friend, Meena, Meena Chandra,' I said loudly, refusing to let go of my ex-friend's hand. There was no way back. No opportunity to scuttle back out the door. Lisa and April blocked the way. The only option was to head further inside. Into the snake pit.

'You look weird. Why do you look weird?' Anthony slurred, taking my hand and pulling me into the living room.

Lisa's voice crowed behind me. 'Look who it is, everyone. India and Meena! And haven't they made an effort! Ennis? Has anyone seen Ennis?'

A scramble as Ennis disentangled himself from a girl on the sofa.

'Ennis – you wanted me to let you know when India got here.'

Ennis had asked after me! Ennis had remembered my name! A smile snuck onto my lips, only to be instantly wiped off as I caught the mouth-crumpling smirk that Tamsin Cooper was shooting in my direction.

Ennis, looking actually really hot although clearly wasted, stumbled towards me, draped his arm round my shoulder, pulled out his phone and snapped. He smelt slightly of sick.

He then lurched to the right and fell asleep at the foot of the sofa.

There was no one left to show an interest in me. No one to protect me.

'The kitchen, now!' Meena hissed into my ear. At least she shared the same survival instinct. We scuttled into the hall, a couple of ninja crabs, and then turned and headed towards the kitchen.

I'd hoped the kitchen would be empty or at least dark. Wrong on both counts. The kitchen table was being used as a makeshift bar and the ceiling spots were full on. Where to go? Where to hide? Eyes scanning left and right in search of sanctuary. The side door – the side door to the garden was fractionally open.

'Come on!' I whispered to Meena. 'Follow me.'

We sidled round Mia Bell and a couple of guys from St Joseph's I recognised, but whose names I didn't know, trying to block out the loudly snort-laughed 'eyebrows' to my left. I was getting paranoid. Just because someone said 'eyebrows' didn't necessarily mean they were talking about me. As Mum says, far too frequently, 'You're not the centre of the universe, India.'

However, the snort came again, this time accompanied by the ever so clearly enunciated, 'India's eyebrows!' Not paranoid. Just perceptive. I've always known Mum was wrong. People *do* spend most of their time thinking about others. And judging them.

The cold air of the garden was a welcome slap in the face. Somewhere under the layers of foundation, highlighter and blusher my actual cheeks would be turning pink. We moved away from the side door and the light that was bleeding out from the kitchen and into the night. There was no moon so it was dark. Properly dark. The kind of dark that almost made me pleased that we weren't taking a night bus back and walking up the road to my house by ourselves, not that I'd admit that to anyone, ever. Halfway down the lawn, we walked straight into a set of garden furniture and, rubbing sore shins, sat down on a couple of the chairs.

Only then did I feel I could breathe again. That my trachea was no longer like one of those paper straws that you over suck and then sort of folds in on itself and only delivers the tiniest bit of Coke Zero.

'What now?' Meena's disembodied voice from my right.

'We wait here for about an hour, let everyone get really drunk so their vision goes and then creep out when no one's looking.'

'OK. Sounds good.'

Good. *Good.* The audacity of her. I snorted. I've never snorted before. Maybe snorting's contagious.

'India, I'm sorry. Please don't stay mad at me. It's not really my fault. After all, CatrinX2000…'

'Never, ever mention that name to me again.'

'Sorry. [Big pause] At least we're alone now.'

'Eh hem.' A disembodied voice from my left. A deep voice. Male. Oh God. No! Was there no escape! No justice in the world!

'Who's there?' I snapped. If it was someone else out to make fun of us, I was going to … Karate chop/sucker punch/do that super-cool-looking pirouette-ending-in-a-flying-kick thing – I don't know what I was going to do, but it wasn't going to be pretty. (To be honest, I was probably just going to cry and with this level of make-up that really wouldn't be pretty either.)

'Sorry. I didn't think anyone else would come out here.' The voice sounded genuinely apologetic. And a little bit scared. 'It's Rich. Rich Evans.'

Rich Evans? Why did I know that name? Oh yes, dimple boy from the Fence.

'Oh, hi!' I replied flatly. Someone else to add to the list of witnesses to my humiliation.

I thought about giving a fake name but then realised he'd been out here longer than us so there was a chance his eyes had adjusted more to the dark and he could see my face and then I'd look like even more of a freak than I did already.

'It's India,' I replied. 'India Smythe, and this is my friend,' I swung my hand in the direction of Meena, accidentally hitting her in the process.

'Ow!' went Meena.

'And this is my friend, Ow Meena Chandra.'

'Hi, India … Meena,' he said. There was a warmth to the way he said 'India' that made me pretty sure that if I could see his face it would be smiling.

There was a silence, but it wasn't too awkward. Not one of those corrosive silences that burrow away at you, perforating your brain until a load of rubbish starts pouring out. This was a comfortable silence.

'What are you doing out here?' I asked after a while.

'Um... Well, I think Anthony might have invited me by accident, maybe got me confused with someone else. I don't seem to know anyone here – it's not really my crowd, I usually hang out with the orchestra gang.' Orchestra *gang*. I managed to swallow a laugh. And not snort. 'Anyway, I got paranoid that people were sort of looking at me and laughing.' He kind of mumbled the last words, his embarrassment plain even in the darkness. 'What about you two? How come you're not inside? You seem more like you'd fit in here.'

Fit in? Here? Tonight? Rich Evans clearly hadn't seen our faces. And for some reason I realised I felt disproportionately pleased about that.

'We, we kind of overdid our make-up,' Meena blurted out. Thanks, Meena. You're really on fire tonight.

'I'm sure you still look really nice,' Rich replied. And there was this sincerity to his voice, which kind of caught me off guard. And I started thinking that he'd never treat a girl badly. That he'd never feel the need to break into a building site and take a dump on the stairs. Or even if he had a minor psychotic episode and did it, he'd never brag about it to a girl on a date.

God, reality check. I was actually picturing me on a date with an orchestra geek. Wake up, India Smythe. Get a grip.

'Thanks for bringing back my homework the other day, by the way,' I said, attempting to snap my brain back into reality. As safe subjects went, totally non-sexy subjects, homework retrieval was about as hairy legs and garlic bread breath as it got.

'No problem,' he replied, laughing. 'I couldn't leave you there looking all flustered and earnest.'

Then he started talking about how once he'd got ketchup on his homework, and his dog, this German shepherd mongrel called Hund that is weirdly partial to ketchup, had actually eaten it and he'd ended up with a detention not because of failing to hand the homework in, but because his teacher thought he was taking the piss with his excuse.

Rich was ridiculously easy to talk to. Meena seemed to think so too as she joined in as well and the conversation just flowed. Moving from topic to topic. Unobstructed by the usual *don't say anything that makes you seem unattractive or tragic* rules. It wasn't normally like this with boys. Before I went on my date with Yan, I spent half an hour in my room writing down a list of suitable conversation topics. *What do you think of Lorde's new single? Are you excited about the new season of Stranger Things? Did you know I'm an eighth French?* (I'm not, actually. I thought I was, but I recently found out that although Great Grandma Maud was born in France, she was otherwise completely English, refused to learn a word of the language and would even turn her nose up at a croissant.) Even with this intensive preparation, the conversation with Yan had been stilted and awkward.

Not like this. We moved onto out-shaming each other with admissions of other embarrassing evenings. Meena launched into a description of her holiday disaster of last year. It was pretty epic. I've heard it a zillion times, but would happily listen to it on repeat, forever. Basically, she'd snuck out at night with her cousin to a beach party where she'd ended up snogging a guy who'd told her that he seemed short because he was standing in a hole and then the full moon had come out from behind a cloud and she'd seen that not only was there no hole, but also that he was also only about eleven. We called her Meenophile paedophile for weeks afterwards. Happy times.

Anyway, Meena was just about to get to the full moon no hole bit when this loud voice boomed out into the garden:

'India! India Smythe! Come here now!'

This, accompanied by peals of cackling laughter.

No. NO. NO!!!!!

Dad.

I wanted to die. To literally press my body into the

grass and watch it disintegrate into the soil and be eaten by worms. All that would be left to show I'd ever been alive would be a particularly verdant patch of grass. Meena checked her phone.

'It's ten forty-five.'

*Ten forty-five!!!!!!!!*

We'd lost track of time. We should have been at the car fifteen minutes ago. That had been the deal. Now the deal was off and Dad was here. HERE.

Life had just hit a new low. It couldn't get any worse.

'India. You'd better not be out there with some BOY!'

It just got worse.

'Dad, I'm coming, OK,' I hissed.

'India? India is that you?'

Oh my God. Was he deaf now? Had his ear hair reached such a density that it now blocked all incoming sound waves?!?

'I'm *coming*!'

I dragged Meena with me and headed towards the irate figure silhouetted against the kitchen side door.

'I'm coming too,' Rich said. 'Looks like you need all the backup you can get.'

I should have told him to stay. To wait in the dark, in safety, but I didn't. There was something attractive, comforting in the idea of a guy providing me with backup. I'd never had a hero before.

Two deep breaths and I stepped into the light.

'INDIA!' came the soprano squeal. 'What the hell have you done to your face?!!!!!!'

I'd forgotten. The hour and a half in the garden in the dark had made me forget all about the horror show that was my face. I raised my hands to cover it with an echoing squeal. If anyone wanted to do a radio play of the night they'd have to press the sound effect for *cat getting run over, slowly*.

'And you!' Dad shouted, staring like a crazed psycho at Rich Evans, who was hovering two steps behind me. 'What were you doing in the dark with my daughter?!!!!'

'Er…' came Rich's eloquent reply. He'd gone a ghostly, clammy white. In-bed-with-severe-flu-with-potential-to-hospitalise level.

'Don't you "er" me, young man! How old are you?'
'Fifteen.'

'Fifteen! Hmmpphhh. Ha! HA! Fifteen!!!!'

Rich looked frozen. Petrified by the mad man that was my dad. Wondering, as was I, why 'fifteen' had prompted this exploding eureka moment.

'I was fifteen once. Don't think for one moment that I don't remember what a fifteen-year-old MAN wants to do to a fourteen-year-old GIRL in a garden in the dark!' Little bits of spit were now flecking out of Dad's mouth and getting caught on his proto-beard. They glistened there like dew on a spider's web.

'It's not like that, Dad,' I hissed back, catching his arm and pulling him deeper into the garden. I had to contain the situation. Shut it down before someone started filming this and it went viral. 'Rich isn't like that. Rich is in the *orchestra*.' Any sane person would understand what I meant. Orchestra = geek = nice boy = safe. I should have realised that Dad was far past sane.

'He's ... a musician ... in ... a ... BAND!' Dad spluttered. 'You were messing about in the dark with a boy from a band!'

'It's not a band!' I yelled 'It's orchestra!'

'Well, actually, I *am* in a band, India.'

'Wind band doesn't count!'

'It's string band.'

Rich wasn't helping. He clearly had no survival instinct. Not the sort of boy to get stranded near a pack of hungry wolves with. *Me? Oh yes, my flesh is really quite tasty and filling.*

It was up to me to salvage the situation.

'Rich wasn't just with me, Dad. Meena was out there too!'

Dad went from red to purple.

'So my daughter wasn't enough, is that it? You needed *more* groupies? Some sort of three-way orgy!?!

Come on you two, we're getting out of here. Away from this pervert and the rest of them.'

There was no fight left in me. I followed Dad into the kitchen, turning at the last moment to flash Rich an apologetic smile and mouth my grovelling apologies.

Rich smiled back and then his mouth dropped open. He'd seen me in the light for the first time. Properly seen me. Oh no, this was the end of our proto-friendship. He was going to hate me too. Reject me too.

But he didn't. He laughed. No snidely. There was no cackle or smirk. He properly belly laughed. And I started laughing too.

Giggling all the way back to the car.

So I'm grounded. For a week. And my phone has been confiscated for a month.

Mum chose to announce this as she flounced into my room in the morning, yanking back the curtains and exposing my tender head to a full-on search beam of late autumn sunlight.

I groaned and Mum made a weird guttural gloating noise.

'Uh huh!'

I think she thought I'd been drinking. That I might have a hangover so this would be the ultimate revenge. I hadn't. I didn't. But still, being half blinded after practically no sleep is never a good thing. I'd crawled into bed just before midnight, after Dad had got back from dropping Meena home – our sleepover abruptly cancelled – but hadn't got to sleep till around four. My brain wouldn't let me. It kept flashing up images of last night's humiliation like one of those toys that look a bit like torches or binoculars that you stare into while pressing a button and you get to see ten different images of Disney princesses/Paris.

*Click*
My face in the bathroom mirror.
*Click*
Lisa's laugh as she opened the door.
*Click*
Anthony asking if anyone had ordered him a hooker.
*Click*
Rich's face as Dad accused him of arranging
an orgy in the back garden.

And so on. Click after click that made me twist and squirm and sweat.

Rich might have laughed about it last night, but

would he really find it so funny in the cold light of day? Would the likes of April and Lisa and their minions forget?

Of course not. Never. Take Harriet Lowe. She ran out of deodorant one day at the start of Year 7 and smelt a bit. Only a bit. For *one* day. She's spent the following three and a bit years as 'Harriet B.O.' There is no forgetting. No escaping. Being grounded is nothing. Has no meaning. My life is over anyway.

Grounded. There was a nice, spherical sound to the word. A flicker of hope sparked in my chest. How comprehensive was this grounding going to be?

'I suppose I won't be allowed to go to school for a while either, so that I don't mix with any more bad influences,' I said pathetically. My voice was weak. My mind was weak. *Save me from myself.*

A snort erupted from Mum's nostrils. Maybe I am genetically destined to be a snorter after all.

'Oh no! You are going to school, India Smythe. You will go to school every morning, on time, no more crawling out of bed last minute, and then you will come straight home every afternoon.'

Goodbye flicker of hope.

'Oh, and India,' she called as a parting shot. 'Wash your pillow.'

I looked down at my pillow and flinched. There were

two dark circles where my eyes had been and red splashes at around cheek and mouth height. A regular Turin shroud (well, if Jesus had listened to Judas's terrible advice and was trying to cultivate an Instagram following.) Normal make-up remover was clearly no match for Catrin2000.

I spent the rest of the weekend feeling how people must when they know a massive hurricane is swirling around just off the coast, building up, ready to hit.

What made it infinitely worse was that I had no means of knowing the full extent of the destruction that would be wrought, or that already had been. I had no phone, not that my phone had Internet anyway. There was no way I could use the 'family computer' with Mum or Dad glued to my shoulder. I wasn't even allowed to use the landline for three days so I couldn't ask Meena or Anna to check. For all I knew, there were pictures of me plastered all over social media, complete with horrific comments, that I knew nothing about. I could have even become a meme and I wouldn't know. Wouldn't know until eight-thirty on Monday morning.

I was initially also massively worried about Meena

and her parents going mad at her. They'd dropped her off at mine for a pizza and movie evening and then she's dropped back home at midnight with scary make-up and a plunging neckline. I waited till Mum and Dad had had their first coffee before asking about it. They're always a lot nicer after that. Mum makes a cappuccino using her Nespresso machine. Her posh friend, Linda, bought one and Mum is the ultimate sheep and now claims she can't possibly drink instant at home. Dad has Nescafé because he says 'it does the job' and I think he thinks it somehow keeps him real. I hovered round, waiting for them to finish their mugs.

'Why are you hovering round, India?' Mum asked. 'You know you're not allowed coffee. It'll damage your developing nervous system. We read all about it in Article Club.'

'I don't want coffee, Mum.' A lie. I drink it all the time at Anna's where her mum makes it with lots of milk and sugar and I really, really fancied some. 'I just wanted to see how Meena's parents were. Check they were OK?'

An unnecessarily slow sip, and then Dad answered.

'I bought Meena some wet wipes from the garage on the way home so she could wipe the stuff off. They were fine. Concerned about you and your 'stomach bug' – ha! – but fine.' At least that was something.

Mum and Dad sentenced me to work all day doing

chores – their own version of community service. Wash the car. Empty the bins. Clean the kitchen. Rake the leaves off the lawn and put them into the special compostable PLAHstic bags. If they could have put me in an orange jumpsuit while I did it they would have before you could say Netflix. OK, orange is more American penal system than British but my parents watch way more American shows and I'm not exactly sure what British prisoners wear or if they even have a uniform. All that springs to mind is striped black and white pyjamas with shot-put balls tied to ankles, but I'm pretty sure that stopped a few centuries back.

They were trying to be mean. To make me 'consider my actions' and 'evaluate my behaviour', but the strange thing was the work actually kind of helped. When your arms are aching, you've got soap suds in your left eye and you accidentally rake over your foot, you can stop thinking for a while. Stop stressing and just focus on the pain instead. Mindfulness 101.

I finished the chores as the light was fading at five and came inside again with two hours still to spare before dinner. Mum and Dad had clearly run out of stuff for me to do, but they weren't going to give up that easily.

'Tidy your room, India,' barked Mum.

'Done,' I replied.

'The car?' attempted Dad.

'Washed and hoovered.'

'Piano?'

'Practised.'

'Because if you don't practise every day for at least half an hour you'll never get anywhere.'

'I've practised.'

Mum's read this article about how you can basically become a genius at anything if you practise it for ten thousand hours.

'I don't know why we pay for expensive piano lessons if you never practise.'

'I said *I've practised* and I don't want you to pay for lessons. I'd prefer it if you didn't pay for lessons.'

'Oh India, you are so ungrateful.'

Aggghhhhhhhhh!!!!!

I wish they didn't make me play the piano. I'm the least musical person in the world and everyone, including my piano teacher, knows it. She won't even enter me for exams as there's always an oral bit where they play various notes and you have to sing them back and there's no chance in hell I'm going to hit them. Mum won't let me give up, as she thinks playing a musical instrument looks good on your UCAS form. And Dad won't let me quit either, as music is really important to him and he still believes I must have some genetic music potential that just needs to be unlocked. Every car trip I am subjected to 'an education in 80s and 90s rock', which takes the form of Dad playing the hits of his youth with a side-serving of rock trivia. Like the fact that *Dancing in the Dark* is about Springsteen's frustration at not being able to break through. Lesser known fact – it also inspired Dad's band's flop: *Can't Get No Hits*. Less metaphorical, more literal.

'Well ... well ... tidy up your dad's Lego set then.'

I should explain, Dad actually does have a Lego set. Mum's posh friend, Linda, is really into mindfulness at the moment, so, obviously, Mum is too. Mum's got all these mindful colouring books and craft sets, but she couldn't get Dad to do that with her, so he took this as an excuse to buy himself a massive set of Lego. Every Sunday while Mum colours/sews/glues for an hour, he locks himself in his study and builds castles and pirate ships and dungeons. This combined with the fact he's said at least once a week throughout my life that he's not disappointed that I'm a girl leads me to conclude that's he's pretty gutted that his only child is lacking a Y chromosome.

Evening came and I went to bed straight after dinner. With a hot water bottle. My bedroom's freezing and it was the closest thing I was going to get to a hug. The whole house is sub-artic nowadays. Our thermostat is set at 18°C downstairs and 16°C upstairs. Normal people's thermostats are not set at 18°C. Normal people's thermostats probably malfunction if you try and type in a one followed by a six. In Anna's house it's 21°C and at Meena's it's 23°C. It might sound pretty anal, but I check these things. I need proof, ammunition. Mum set ours lower last year 'because it's better for the environment' but she still has air-freighted blueberries for breakfast about once a week and she 'coincidentally' decided to freeze us the exact same day that she read this long article about how turning down the thermostat 'just a couple of degrees' is the best way to boost your metabolic rate and burn fat. You don't have to be a moustachioed Belgian detective to grasp what's going on.

Anyway, I've given up trying to convince her to warm up our ice house and instead have to wait till they go out, then heat-blast the place for a few hours. If you think about it, I'm probably the only reason our pipes don't freeze in winter…

I left the house early: 8:05am. I'm not a good morning person so this was a feat that has never been achieved before, and will probably never happen again.

Mum and Dad shot each other smug looks over toast triangles as I walked out, as if their incredible parenting had finally taught me some discipline and inspired a new, super-diligent me. It was nothing like that. And I've always been pretty diligent, anyway. I get good grades because I want good grades because I want to go to uni and get a good job, but that's not something you need to wake before the birds to manage. It's not like I've ever seen anyone on *Dragons' Den* saying, *The secret to success is hanging around on the pavement outside school, waiting for the gates to open. It's key networking time.*

This morning wasn't about grades, obviously. I needed to talk to someone who hadn't been banished to the Dark Ages. I needed to find out how bad the situation really was before entering the war zone a.k.a. our classroom. Meena was no use. Like me, she always crawls through the gates just as the bell is ringing.

Anna, however, is different.

Anna is a morning person.

I rounded the corner from the High Street onto St Leonard's Way, Anna's route to school, and lay in wait.

As if by clockwork, at 8:15am Anna marched by. Backpack on two shoulders (to evenly distribute weight and prevent back pain in middle age), fleece scarf (for protection against tiny, slightly cold breeze) and hat (pulled firmly down over head to minimise heat loss rather than hitched slightly back to reveal a more flattering inch of hair, swept over stylishly, like a fringe). Ah, Anna. I felt all warm and fuzzy. There's nothing fake about Anna. What you see is what you get. She's worth a million Aprils or Lisas. She also has an iPhone with a really high data allowance.

'India!' Anna called out as she saw me. Genuinely delighted. Her face then crumpled in concern. 'Are you OK? Meena called yesterday to see if I'd heard from you as she couldn't get hold of you.' [Dramatic pause.] 'She told me about Saturday night.' Anna's voice had dropped to a whisper.

Oh God. If even Anna, who seemed to possess zero social barometer, could tell it was bad, it was bad. It was properly bad.

'How bad is it?' I asked.

'I don't know,' Anna replied, earnestly. 'It's hard to tell.'

'Go on.'

At least Anna would keep this unemotional. She'd tell me the facts. Apply logic. Determine a conclusion. She'd be like a computer running an analysis of the problem.

'No videos that I've seen but you were in the back of lots of photos, Meena only a couple.'

'Uh huh.'

Just the word 'photo' sent all the downy hairs at the back of my neck horizontal. My face. My hideous, horror-doll's face had been captured on film. Worse, it had been captured in H.D. pixels and was floating about in the ether so couldn't be cut up/burnt/deleted.

'But you looked OK,' Anna continued. 'Your expressions were all weird. Your mouth a bit open, eyes a bit vacant, back a bit hunched over, but nothing terrible.'

So I looked like a less intelligent Hunchback of Notre Dame. Excellent.

'What about comments?'

'Pretty good, actually. Lots of "Have u seen India?" "Doesn't she look AMAZING!"'

Sarcasm. The computer doesn't understand sarcasm.

'Then there was this one other photo.'

My heart sank. This would be it. The one close-up. The ticket to solitary confinement.

'Show me.'

Anna flicked through her phone.

'Here.'

Half our class had shared it. It had one hundred and forty-three likes. And there it was: the photo Ennis had taken before he passed out. His arm round my shoulders. His eyes half closed but in a kind of sexy way. I was looking at the camera. Side on. My good side. My mouth wasn't open. My eyes weren't vacant. My back wasn't hunched. I looked OK. I looked more than OK. My eyes popped, my cheekbones sliced, my lips looked like they'd been stung by a full-on hive of bees. Floating around the ether was probably the best photo of me that had ever been taken!

Underneath were three comments.

The all-important comments.

I steeled myself.

Lisa: a heart and then a crying with laughter face.

Hmmm. The crying with laughter face definitely wasn't good, but what did the heart mean? Maybe she loved the way I looked? Or … or maybe she loved my humiliation? Loved laughing at me?

April: three crying with laughter faces.

That was not good. No positive spin there.

Maybe I should fake really bad period pains and go home now. Jasmine Thompson fakes them every time there's swimming and Ms Hunter is too dense to realise that you can't biologically have your period every single week.

Ennis: a symbol that looked a bit like an explosion or a spark.

That wasn't usually used. Fire, yes. Fire was easy. Fire would mean hot. But an explosion? What did that mean? What the hell did that mean?!?

I looked at Anna for help, but she looked back blankly, clearly out of her depth and aware of it. But that wasn't going to stop her from having a go.

'Um. Taken together I can only assume you all had a fun time, maybe around some sort of camp fire? Or perhaps an electrical appliance overheated and exploded?'

No help whatsoever.

It felt like I'd just watched someone take a Rorschach inkblot test, where the answer reveals more about the person interpreting it than anything else. Spark à fire à camping. If I'd let her continue we probably would have ended up with à Mountain Warehouse à brilliant practical clothes.

I couldn't complain, though. I shouldn't have looked to her for help in the first place. It was like asking a Premier League footballer to sort out the situation in the Middle East. *Um … I've got it! Why not have a football match?* That said, maybe fielding a mixed team of Israeli and Palestinian players who had to work together to make it through to the final could achieve what decades of politicians haven't. If not, it could make a very successful worthy film. Maybe I should write to my MP? Or a production company. Be something for the UCAS form. Grade 2 Piano, third team Netball, oh, and genius behind innovative Middle East peace solution/Oscar-winning movie.

'India?'

Snap! I was back in reality. I had to get a grip. Minutes were ticking by and I was daydreaming about Middle East peace rather than the far more important and pressing issue of how to find out the true meaning behind Ennis's emoji.

I had to locate Meena and fast.

Brriiiiinnnnnnggggg.

The bell announcing the start of school. It was hideously loud as usual, probably because bells, fire alarms and safety lockdowns come under the remit of our Deputy Head, Mrs Bruton, who is massively old and deaf. To her ears it was probably no more than a gentle dove's coo. Anyway, the important thing was that the bell had rung and I had five minutes to work out where I stood and still get to registration in time to avoid a late mark, detention and the subsequent double parental heart attack.

Me and Anna were stood behind the yew bush just inside the school gates, prime spotting position. Mid-ring, we saw Meena and pounced.

'What the...' came Meena's indignant squeal as I

pulled her aside and behind the bush. If uni doesn't work out, I could always go into kidnapping. I think I have a certain flair.

'OK, crazy lady,' Meena yelped. 'What's going on?' And then she registered me properly and a horrible look of understanding passed across her forehead. Like suddenly she understood why I was acting mental. My fears were founded.

'Come on,' Anna hissed. 'We'll get a detention if we stand around. We need to walk and talk.'

The four of us started speed walking towards classroom 10J. Even our speech accelerated. All clipped sentences. No small talk. It was like we were in an episode of *The West Wing*. It was almost pretty cool.

'Ennis's spark?'

'Simple. You're hot,' Meena fired back.

A smile swam towards my lips.

'Or...' Meena continued. *Why did there have to be an or*!?! 'Taking into account the context of the evening, a more likely interpretation is an exploded reputation. Total social destruction.'

The smile drowned. I felt sick. Properly nauseous. This was worse than Rameses Revenge at Chessington. Damn Meena. Damn her. It was all her fault and yet she'd somehow managed to avoid the fallout. Close-ups, emojis and all.

'So what's the plan?' Anna, getting us back on track.

Silence. Silence all around. What's the point of having two best friends if they're both zero use in emergencies? I should get a dog. At least you can pat a dog and it doesn't watch YouTube tutorials.

The door to 10J was now five metres ahead and starting to close. The sound of Mrs Johnson's voice beginning to take the register reached out towards us.

'You could just skip school today,' Meena whispered. 'Fake ill for a week. It'll pass in a week.'

'Harriet B.O.,' I whispered back.

Meena had no answer for this. There was no answer. I was facing a stark choice. I had to either run away from home and start again someplace else with an entirely new identity or I had to walk through that door and style it out.

I chose to walk.

Mondays start with whole school hymn practice. On the upside, this meant I managed to go straight from my seat for registration, to the front of the line out the door, to the hall and, through this cunning manoeuvring, was able to avoid Lisa and April's clutches for another forty-five minutes. On the down side, this meant being crammed into a hall that smells like dried parmesan (it really does – we did a smell comparison test last week, Anna smuggled some cheese in) with seven-hundred-plus other students while Mrs Trent, our Head of Music, bashes out songs on the piano. And intermittently humiliates people.

The rule, the crucial rule, for hymn practice is DON'T TALK. Normally, in assemblies, you can get away with the odd whispered conversation. A bit of 'check out Mrs Hazel's tragic velvet hairband, she looks horrific' or 'I'm getting more of a cheddary vibe today' without any repercussions. Worst case scenario, you'll end up on the receiving end of a particularly loud SHUUUSSSHHHH!

Mrs Trent is different.

Mrs Trent is a witch.

A witch with Daredevil-level super hearing. This morning, in the fear and horror and confusion of the whole emoji business, I forgot this. Quite how, I'll never know. Maybe the stress of everything had given me a mini stroke and stopped a portion of my brain from functioning. Anyway, halfway through the first chorus of *All Things Bright and Beautiful* I broke the rule. I spoke. Quietly. Really just a whisper. I'd seen

April and Lisa out the corner of my eye to my right and my stomach had flipped and I needed reassurance. I needed a friend.

'It'll be OK won't it?' I whispered to Anna, next to me. Anna looked stunned and edged away, distancing herself from the talking moron. 'It's just a photo,' I went on, hating the needy whine to my voice. If Anna could have changed rows she would have. I think I saw her knees come up as if she was preparing to bum shuffle her way out of there. It didn't matter. If that had been her plan, it was already too late. Somehow, through the loud clangs of the piano and the semi-yelling singing voices, Daredevil-level had managed to detect the low undertones of speech and, using her dark magic, had pinpointed its source.

Abruptly, Mrs Trent stopped playing and slammed down the piano lid. Voices petered out and there was a static electricity in the air. I imagine there was a very similar atmosphere during the French Revolution, right before a public beheading. The thrill and fear of knowing that someone else was going down mingled with the relief that this time it wasn't going to be you. Sweet and Salty popcorn.

Mrs Trent stood up and prowled down the middle aisle. Maybe she hadn't heard me? Maybe someone else had been speaking louder?

'India Smythe!' Her voice ripped the air apart. *Bollocks.* 'Stand up!'

I got shakily to my feet. A newborn lamb testing its legs for the first time. While a rather hungry wolf watched.

'So you think you're above hymn practice, do you?'

'No, Mrs Trent,' I mumbled.

'Think you're SO good you don't need to practise, is that it?'

'No, Mrs Trent.' *Help, where was this going? Was I even supposed to be answering these rhetorical questions?*

'Well, maybe if you're SO good you can teach the rest of us. Follow me to the front.'

*God, no. No. NO! This is where this was going. Help me someone. Lightning strike me now.*

'Stand on the stage.'

I did as instructed, half expecting someone to wheel a guillotine out from the wings.

'I'm going to play the chorus again and India here, who is TOO GOOD to practise, will show us all how it's done.'

My whole skin broke out in goosebumps; I think I even had goosebumps on my eyelids, although that may be biologically impossible, and I started sweating like someone dumped in the desert without deodorant. Even if I survived this, from here on I was going to be known as India B.O. anyway.

I can't sing. I literally can't sing. At primary school when I was a camel in the Year 6 nativity play, Miss Smith had encouraged me to 'say the words rather than sing them'. She didn't say that to anyone else in the class. I checked. I can make some low notes, but high notes are unreachable for me. I'll aim for them but my voice will crack and squeal and I'm like a thirteen-year-old boy. I stared at the cross on the wall above the piano. *Come on, Jesus. You're supposed to like children. 'Suffer little children and forbid them not to come unto me.' Surely you can't sit/hang there and watch as a girl who's already on the verge of a breakdown from extreme stress gets further tortured? How about some smiting? Any possibility you could make your dad go all Old Testament on Mrs Trent?*

Apparently he couldn't.

Mrs Trent started to play.

'Sing, India,' she yelled.

I started. 'All THings bri-ght and beau-TI-ful,'

'Louder, I can't hear you!'

'All crea-TURes gre-at and SM-all.' My voice was all over the place. I found that if I squinted slightly I could make the faces, the seven hundred faces staring at me, go away. Turn them into a pinky brown blur.

'Stay in tune!'

'All thIN-gs wi-SE and won-DER-ful.'

'Come on!'

'The LO-rd Go-D made th-EM all.'

I don't know how I managed to walk back to my seat again. I think as soon as I stepped off the stage my mind was busy trying to destroy memory cells. A survival instinct.

No one laughed at me as we filed out of assembly. No one stared or pointed or cough insulted – you know, the lamest and cowardliest form of insult, when someone half covers up what they're saying with a barking cough.

*Co-MORON-ugh.* No one even mentioned the damp patches on my shirt. Instead, everyone looked shocked. Like they'd been forced to watch an execution so bloody it'd put them off their baguettes.

Meena was the only person to say anything.

'Wow,' she managed.

'Yup,' I replied, trying to sound nonchalant and failing dismally. 'This is really not my day.'

I felt April and Lisa's eyes on my back all through first period. They were like hot lasers, searing flesh. But I didn't dare turn around. Better to feel the burn than face the enemy. I'd already been scarred this morning. Another full-on confrontation and humiliation would destroy me.

I obviously couldn't concentrate on anything. Luckily, it was Geography so there wasn't really anything to concentrate on anyway. It's such a non-subject. It takes really exciting things like volcanoes and earthquakes and reduces them to beyond tedious case studies. And it's the terminology. *Andesitic magma*. It's enough to make the worst insomniac go full-on sleeping beauty.

Today we had to draw four annotated diagrams to show the gradual formation of an oxbow lake. As the world's about to flood from global warming and America and Russia are starting another arms race, I'm pleased to see that Mr Morretts has got his educational priorities straight. *How are we going to stop sea levels wiping out the London Borough of Lambeth? I don't know, but if the seas fill up the rivers there might be some more oxbow lakes formed. Let's talk about how exactly that would happen.*

At least there are no sets, so I got to sit between Meena and Anna and felt cocooned and protected from both sides. We usually spend the fifty minutes waiting to see how long it takes for Mr Morretts to turn purple and kick someone out for 'inappropriate behaviour'. Why he decided to teach in an all girls' school is beyond me. He can't handle it, he really can't. There's a sweepstake on at the moment for who can get kicked out fastest. Sophie is the current record holder at seven seconds. Last week she sat at the front and kept making eyes at him and leaning forward with her top button undone. You could see the palpitations though his checked shirt.

No one messed around this morning, though. It was like everyone's attention was elsewhere. Waiting for the fallout between me and Lisa and April. Waiting to discover the true meaning of the explosion emoji.

'That's it for today.' Mr Morretts' voice overlapped with the end of lesson bell. It was infused with relief. He'd got through a lesson unscathed. 'Homework is to finish the drawings.'

No one wrote it down. I don't think anyone was listening. Everyone was watching me. Watching as Lisa and April stood up and stalked towards me like a pair of conjoined twins. No facial expressions (but then there often weren't to reduce possible wrinkle formation) so their emotions were unreadable.

I hadn't registered before how bendy they are. They

kind of sway as they walk. Left. Right. Left. Right. I can never get past BAGA 3 in gym, whereas they probably accidentally slip into the splits whenever they bend down to pick up the TV remote.

'Hello, India,' Lisa began. Think *The Jungle Book* snake. The old cartoon one. I kind of expected her eyes to start spinning, all psychedelic.

'Hello,' echoed April.

'Hi guys,' I mumbled back, wincing at my 'guys'. Wishing I could pluck that 'guys' out from the air and reinsert it back into my mouth.

Then the miracle occurred.

Lisa smiled.

And April smiled.

They both smiled.

At *me*.

I did a subtle neck swivel to check that no boys were standing directly behind me, but they weren't.

'Hope you enjoyed the party,' Lisa continued, the smile still in place.

How to respond? How the hell to respond? *Of course I didn't enjoy the party, you pair of evil dolls, because you mocked me all night so I had to hide in the garden until my dad picked me up and shamed me even more.*

I went with, 'Um. Yeah.'

All the time I was just thinking *what's their plan here*? Is this the slow-burn take down? Like that time when they were super friendly to Emily Button who collects toothpaste tops and then, three hours later stole her glasses so she was left a stranded mole for the rest of the afternoon.

'Well, Ennis enjoyed it too.' April literally purred this at me.

'Cool,' I replied, trying to keep my voice steady.

'He enjoyed seeing *you* at the party.'

'Cool,' I replied. I was turning into a robot. A particularly cheap robot with a very limited vocabulary.

'India!' April's tone changed. Sharpened. 'Keep up. Your moron routine might work on Ennis but it doesn't cut it with us. Ennis thinks you're hot. Ennis wants to go out with you.'

'Um,' *don't say cool, don't say cool*, '…epic.'

*Epic?*

*Why the hell didn't I just say cool?!?*

'India,' Lisa pulled me closer and lowered her tone. 'I don't think you quite understand the situation. Ennis. Wants to go. On a date. With you.'

'Yay!' I managed feebly.

'Don't mess this up,' April hissed. 'If you mess this up it reflects badly on us. He said to message him.'

'My phone…'

'Don't bother us with the details.'

'No, seriously. I … don't have my phone right now. I sort of need his actual number. Written down.'

April rolled her eyes at me, tapped at her phone and then scribbled on an orange Post-it note from her bag.

'Here.' She thrust the Post-it towards me.

'Organise a date with Ennis,' Lisa instructed. 'Make it a success. That's it.' They swivelled bendily in the other direction and off they went again. Left. Right. Left. Right.

A flick of hair and a final swivel – 'Oh and you can start having lunch with us if you want.'

At least that cleared up the whole meaning of the spark thing. Ennis thought I was hot. Ennis wanted to go on a date with me. Now the issue was – did I want to go on a date with him?

'Of course you do!' Meena semi-exploded at first break. 'You have literally no choice here. A guy like Ennis wants to go on a date; Lisa and April tell you to go on said date – you have no choice. You have been invited to the top level. You do not turn down the top level and survive. It'd be like being offered a free upgrade on an aeroplane or something and then saying you'd prefer to stay in economy and pay for a disgusting long-life sandwich. The first class people wouldn't get it. And they'd be angry.'

My head was reeling from this rubbish analogy. The people in first class would probably be pleased, wouldn't they? Fewer people = more space + more free champagne.

Then it was Anna's turn. Anna clinched it. Totally unintentionally.

'Don't listen to them,' she said firmly. 'It's up to you, India. Lots of people warned me against joining the orchestra, said it's not cool, that people might look down on me, but that's not been the case at all. Orchestra is *so* cool. You meet properly interesting people and everyone's happy to be themselves. I say don't go out with Ennis. Call that nice guy, what was his name? Rich?'

'Rich Evans,' I said quietly.

'OK, I say call Rich Evans instead and be one of us.'

I turned pale. White as a ghost. As if I'd taken all the toothpaste from Emily Button's discarded toothpaste tubes and rubbed it onto my face. Why the hell was I hesitating? Anna had shown me how stark the choice facing me was. Go on a date with Ennis and ascend to stratospheric social heights or turn him down, go for someone like Rich Evans and sink to orchestra-level, despised and tormented by Lisa and April for the rest of my school life.

'I'm going to arrange a date,' I whispered.

'Good decision.' Meena looked visibly relieved. 'You'll only have to keep him interested for another month and then maybe you'll get invited to Lisa's Christmas Party. They have an ice sculpture. Did I tell you they had an ice sculpture?'

'You're doing it again,' I sighed. 'You have a problem.'

'Sorry,' Meena replied, sheepishly. 'It's just that it's such an amazing party!' A cloud crossed her face. 'What about the whole no phone thing? How are you going to call Ennis? Do you want to borrow mine?' Meena held her phone out towards me.

'No.' I was tired now. Emotionally drained. The last thing I wanted was to message Ennis with my best friends peering over my shoulder and offering advice. Forcing advice down my throat like a French goose farmer. I'd asked for his number for a reason. For privacy. 'I'll call him later.'

'How?' Anna this time.

'We have a landline. I'll wait till my parents are out then call him on that.'

Two mouths widened to perfect circles before hitting the floor.

'What? I'd have to talk to him on the date anyway.'

The mouths still hadn't closed.

I'd had it, so I started to walk away.

Meena's voice chased after me.

'Aren't you going to thank me?'

*What? WHAT?*

'I was right, wasn't I? It *is* more important to look good in photos than in reality, isn't it?'

Mum could tell that today had taken it out of me and for once didn't have a go at me when she got back from work. There's normally always something. I'll hear the front door slam, a scuffly sound as she climbs out of her heels and into her UGG slippers, an exaggerated sigh and then the accusations begin.

*India – you've left your bag in the middle of the floor.*

*India – you've hung up your coat at a weird angle.*

*India – you've put the milk back in the fridge wrong.*

Seriously. Once she had this massive go at me because the milk handle was facing towards the inside of the door rather than out for easy access, so I'd potentially slowed down her emergency tea making by three milliseconds. It's not even that she was in a caffeine withdrawal spiral and desperate for her next fix – she only ever drinks decaf after four anyway. And the hassle is always preceded or followed by some reference to her having 'been at work all day' even though her work sounds like loads more fun than school and just seems to consist of swanning from marketing meeting to marketing meeting and 'brainstorming ideas'. I would much prefer to brainstorm ideas on how to make an essay on *Of Mice and Men* really great than actually having to write the thing.

Today, however, she said her normal *India* – but then stopped. Maybe my face still hadn't returned to its usual, slightly pink colour.

'Is everything OK?'

How to answer? Obviously, I could tell her what was going on. About how I'd been frantically trying to decipher emojis on Instagram, about how I'd been humiliated in assembly, about how I now had to call one of the two most rated guys at St Joseph's and not make a total fool of myself, but what would be the point? One potential outcome would be a bit of sympathy, a hastily baked cake and a hug.

(Mum's a rubbish health-obsessed cook, but a brilliant baker and an avid fan of *The Great British Bake Off*. She even has one of those ovens with the retractable doors for easy cake insertion. She is also prone to pepper her conversation with weird baking metaphors that no one else uses – *he gave me a glare that could curdle batter/she didn't make his soufflé rise if you know what*

*I mean.* I've tried telling her that they're not real sayings, but she just laughs as if *I'm* the crazy lady.)

But just as likely an outcome would be Mum becoming even more convinced that social media and phones were the spawn of the Devil, her storming into school to have a go at Mrs Trent, and then her finding Ennis's number and calling him to say that her daughter wasn't ready for boys, thank you very much.

'Everything's fine, Mum,' I replied.

She didn't buy it for a minute, but what else could she say?

'OK, well… I'll whip up a quick lemon drizzle.'

One out of three wasn't so bad.

There was no opportunity to call Ennis this evening. Dad was working late so he wasn't a problem, but Mum was in all night. Sat in front of the TV, wearing active wear, watching *The Good Place*. She has all these super-expensive patterned legging and top combos that she almost exclusively wears to watch TV and have coffee with her similarly dressed friends on Thursdays and Fridays, when she doesn't work. Like just wearing the clothes is enough. Like they have an inbuilt calorie repulsion field. *Another Brownie? I shouldn't, but, wait a minute, I'm wearing extreme fitness clothes, so why not?*

Not only are Mum and her friends wearing these clothes inappropriately, but what they can't seem to grasp is that, unless you have a boy's bum and legs up to your armpits, leggings without a long top or jumper is a terrible look. But it's short jumpers all the way for the fifty-year-old mums, so there's nothing to block my view of Karen/Linda/Jo/Mum's 'sculpted' bum. It's vaguely indecent. I had to hide her latest active wear catalogue as it had a 'day to night' section featuring women wearing leggings out to a bar in the evening. I didn't want her getting ideas. It's for her own good.

I had no choice. I had to call Ennis tonight. April, Lisa and Meena all had a massive go at me today at school for not calling him already and I needed to get them off my back. And tonight was the perfect opportunity – no one was around to overhear. Mum and Dad were both going to be out at some lame-o pub quiz (they and Tara from down the street's parents belong to a team called 'The Whizz Kidz' – it's so tragic) so this was as good as it was going to get.

I stared at the phone. Sat in its silver-grey holder on the hall console table. How could this simple, ancient object be freaking me out so much? It wasn't really any different to a mobile. A massive brick mobile from the eighties. It'd be just like calling someone on my normal phone whilst simultaneously strengthening my biceps. But then I started thinking: when's the last time I actually called, not messaged, but *spoke* to someone on my phone? Mum doesn't count. Which left … no one. Bar the odd emergency call to Anna or Meena and the annual thank you for my awful Christmas present call to Nan, I talk to NO ONE on the phone. This was going to be a disaster. A travesty.

I began to hyperventilate. Where did Mum keep the brown paper bags? In movies, if someone starts hyperventilating there's always a brown paper bag on hand. Movies are so factually inaccurate.

Time to get a grip. I had to relax. Become confident, bubbly India.

Step 1: Get warm.

People are less stressed out in hot countries. Plus more confident, more passionate. I needed to channel Gloria from *Modern Family*. Minus the accent. The accent might freak him out a bit.

I marched halfway up the stairs and stopped in front

of the thermostat. Clutching the dial, I twisted it to the right, watching the digits spin. 21°C. No. That wasn't going to cut it. A task like this required something special. If there'd ever been a need for a 23°C night, this was it.

Step 2: Sugar boost.

I was flagging and needed to perk up. I was about as bubbly as a can of Coke Zero that had been opened three days ago and then left on a radiator. Mum says I react badly to sugar. That I'm unusually sensitive. But tonight was an unusual evening and if I ended up on a bit of a high, so what? Which way to go? There wasn't really a choice. It had to be hot chocolate. I reached up to the cupboard and pulled down the largest mug I could find, turning it so that 'World's Best Dad' faced away from me. Three heaped teaspoons of economy cocoa powder, four teaspoons of sugar, half a pint of milk and thirty seconds in the microwave later, it was ready. Almost. Final touches were some squirty whipped cream (which is frankly worth putting on even if you don't intend to eat it and are just going to scoop it off and chuck it in the sink as the act of pressing down the nozzle and watching the cream bubble out everywhere is so cool) and three large marshmallows. Time to let it work its magic.

*Gulp. Delicious. Damn, I make good hot chocolate. But not ready to call. Not remotely ready.*

*Gulp and marshmallow for luck. Feeling a bit better. I'm not sure why I'm so worried. I'm pretty cool, really.*

*Gulp and second marshmallow. Ennis is lucky that I'm going to call him. He is so lucky! I'm also a great dancer.*

*Gulp. Only one marshmallow left. It looks lonely. Like a marshmallow floating on a sea of cream. It needs a friend. Maybe a Lego friend? Don't worry little iceberg, I'll unlock Dad's study and get you a Lego friend... Got one! ... Look – he's got brown hair. He looks quite serious. A bit like Patrick Swayze in the bit in* Dirty Dancing *when he's worried about his pregnant non-girlfriend dancer. Hey Patrick Swayze, why are you stranded on an iceberg? Is it because no one knows who you are any more? I still like you. I'll rescue you.*

*Gulp. Patrick Swayze's drowning in the final two centimetres of hot chocolate and my head hurts.*

I put down the hot chocolate and had a slice of bread and butter to stabilise my blood sugar levels.

I checked the time. Eight-thirty. I had to do this. Stop procrastinating. If I waited much longer it'd be nine and then nine-thirty and then ten and it might seem like I was making some sort of late night booty call. I fished the orange Post-it note out of my bag and carried it and the phone through to the lounge a.k.a. war room. Should I make a list of things to say? No, that hadn't worked with Yan. I was fourteen. I had to act fourteen. I was just a fourteen-year-old girl calling a fifteen-year-old boy. Nothing strange; nothing unusual.

With shaking hands I dialled the number.

It rang.

Bring Bring…

*Maybe he's out?*

Bring Bring…

*Or maybe he's just not going to answer.*

Bring Bring…

*It'll probably go straight to answer phone… I should have prepared an answer phone message. Why didn't I prepare an answer phone message??*

Bring Bring…

*Should I say hey or hi?*

Bring Bring…

*Hey… Hi … they both sound rubbish Agghhhh!*

The message cut in.

'It's Ennis. You know what to do. *BEEP.*'

This was it. This was crunch time.

Breathe…

'[*Weird deep breathing sound*] Hey … hi … hello, um, Ennis, this is me, um, India. Yes, well, Lisa and April said to call you, so here I am, calling you HA HA HA! Um, well, bye then.'

I replaced the phone in the handset and sat there, frozen.

I don't think that could have gone any worse. Ten out of ten for total weirdo loser message. The winning combo of deep breathing, followed by the triple hello greeting, followed by moron garble and laughing for no reason is not going to make me look like a total freak at all. He'll never call me back. He'll never want to even hear my name again. I failed. I totally, completely messed up. Meena will be so disappointed in me.

Then a horrible thought struck: what if he plays someone my message?!? I hope he doesn't play anyone my message. I hope he doesn't play Lisa and April my message.

I didn't move from the sofa for the next two and a half hours. I couldn't even bring myself to watch more than two episodes of *13 Reasons Why*, that's how low I was feeling. The next fully conscious moment was Mum and Dad arriving back, initially all drunk and giggly.

The drunk and giggly soon evaporated. The transition from naughty school children to members of the Spanish Inquisition took all of three seconds.

Dad:    India, why are you still up, it's a school night?!
Mum:   India, it's boiling in here. Have you touched the thermostat?… India, it's set at 23°C!!!!! Do you want to get diabetes?
Me:      Meena's house is always at 23°C!
Mum:   Well, Meena's mum isn't exactly petite is she?

Me:     She's got a thyroid problem!

Mum:   But what caused the thyroid problem?

*I give up. I completely give up.*

Dad:    Why's my study door unlocked?... India – there are Lego men everywhere!... Let me see that... Oh, India!!! Why's there a Lego man in the bottom of that cup? And what's the phone doing in here? You haven't been making late night ... calls have you?

I could literally see the word *BOOTY* can-can-ing across his forehead in five centimetre high neon lights.

Dad:    It wasn't to that pervert from the party, was it?

I stopped answering and started climbing the stairs to bed. There's only so much a girl can take.

And so ends another normal night in the Smythe household.

I was going to miss breakfast, I just wasn't feeling hungry, but Mum wouldn't let me leave the house until I'd finished a bowl of porridge topped with grimbo toasted pumpkin seeds and açai berries.

'They're a superfood, India. There're so many bugs around at this time of year. This is nature's protection.' I'm not convinced that an açai berry could really take out a cold/flu/norovirus but the porridge didn't actually taste too bad. Not *let's break into a house and risk the wrath of three differentially sized bears* good, but good enough.

Mum also returned my phone, which was a bonus. She'd read an article about a kid being abducted in some different part of the country and was worried someone might try and nab me on the way to school. I had to promise to text as soon as I reached the school gates.

We had Art first thing and as we began the trek to the new art block after registration, Meena and Anna both jumped me, desperate to hear every single juicy detail of my 'asking Ennis out' as Meena put it.

'I wasn't asking him out!' I replied indignantly. '*He* wants to go on a date with *me*!'

'So, what *did* you ask him?' Meena demanded.

'Nothing. I didn't ask him anything…'

'Oh, that's a big mistake,' Anna interrupted. 'It's always good to ask boys questions. They like it when you show interest.' *Like you know! 'Excuse me, orchestra boy, precisely what type of wood is your violin made from?'*

'What exactly did you say, India?' Meena repeated, impatiently. 'I want to hear it. Word for word.'

'Yes, tell us, India. Tell us.'

I was feeling claustrophobic from their faces pressing into mine, stealing my air, and I couldn't think straight from the lack of oxygen. I dropped the cocky façade and told them the truth. I didn't need to dig deep into my memory. The words were seared into the longterm section. I'd need a lobotomy to forget.

'OK. OK. Don't laugh. Promise you won't laugh?'

Solemn nods all round.

'I said: "Hey … hi … hello, um, Ennis, this is me, um, India. Yes, well, Lisa and April said to call you, so here I am, calling you HA HA HA! Um, well, bye then."'

Anna was the first to react.

'Oh.'

Meena made it past a single word. 'God, India, that's terrible. That's the worst message I've ever heard!'

I expected her to go all mental at me for ruining her chances at getting good boys and invites to Lisa's party and stuff through me, but instead she doubled up and started laughing. Then, a second later, we were all laughing and there's such an echo in the new art block corridor that our cackles were bouncing off the walls and round us and the whole thing suddenly didn't seem so bad.

We were still laughing when we walked into the main studio, which by the way is pretty cool – loads of big windows, which flood the room with light. A sort of cathedral to paint.

I like Art. And I'm pretty good at it. If you want a charcoal sketch of an old flower pot to look remarkably like an old flower pot, then I'm your girl. Mr Major loves my work. Every other week I'll have something in one of the frames that line the art block corridor and in class he'll often hold up my work as an example of what to aspire to. I pretend to be all embarrassed, but really, inside, I'm super proud and glowing. It's not like I want to be an artist or anything. Stacey's mum's an artist and they live in a tiny flat and always seem to be massively stressed about money, but I like the fact that moving to Paris and living in romantic bohemian squalor might be an option for me.

But Mr Major wasn't here this morning. A new teacher stood in his place. A thin woman in her twenties with a streak of red hair in the midst of black curls, drowning in a shapeless grey dress and oversized green plastic glasses. I instantly knew I wasn't going to like her. There was just something about her. Like I could smell it. Eau de self-importance. She looked like the sort of person who'd pretend not to like Paris. Who'd claim to prefer Whitechapel. Mum took me to a gallery in Whitechapel once when she was trying to break into the gang of 'creative' mums at school. We both agreed it was pretty overrated and Mum had her hand in her pocket, clutching her attacker alarm all the time. She nearly had a heart attack when she looked up flat prices on Rightmove afterwards.

'Hello class, my name is Ms Roberts.'

'Good morning, Ms Roberts,' everyone chorused back while Meena whispered, 'Hey … hi … hello,' in my ear. I cracked up, I couldn't help it, and earned myself an evil from the new teacher. It didn't bother me too much. I knew I could get her back on side when she saw my work.

'Mr Major has been taken ill,' she continued, 'so I'm going to be your art teacher until he recovers. This is my first teaching position. After Goldsmiths…' she let the word hang in the air for a few seconds as if waiting for us to swoon at her artistic success – *ooohhh Goldsmiths* – 'I ran my own studio in Whitechapel for a while,' *of course you did*, 'and have now decided to share my knowledge with the artists of the future – you!' Cue dramatic hand sweep of the room. Meena shook silently next to me.

'Today, as our inspiration, we take a simple sprig of ivy.' With further dramatic flourishes, she plonked pieces of ivy down on each bench at intervals. 'Interpret as you will. All media are welcome. There are no rules in my art room!'

It was as if she was performing in her own self-penned play: *The Inspirational Art Teacher. Act One.*

Meena opted for paint, because, let's face it, paint is fun; Anna went old school with a 2B pencil and I reached for my trusty charcoal. Time to put this newbie in her place.

Forty minutes later, I'd finished an incredibly life-like sketch. The stem curled round, and the leaves twisted and spread, the whole thing almost 3-D jumping out of the page at you without the need for those rubbish cinema glasses that just end up giving you a headache.

'Wow!' said Anna. 'You're so annoyingly good at this!'

I looked at hers. It was OK, but a bit bland with dodgy perspective. Meena's was hysterical. Green printed triangles joined together with a string that looked like blue barbed wire.

'What can I say? I was feeling creative!' she laughed.

'I'm sure it has a very significant meaning,' I giggled back.

'Yes. Yes,' she agreed, channelling pretentious art

critic. 'Blue meets green. The environmental threat to the ocean.'

'Interesting, I was thinking of the blue-blooded royals protecting the countryside yet damaging abstract art.'

We sat around for a few minutes, stroking imaginary beards and nodding our heads earnestly.

Mr Major always used to walk round the room offering advice while we worked. Helping mix colours or giving tips on technique. Ms Roberts, however, had just sat herself down at her desk and started knitting something with mustard coloured wool.

'What is a teacher, anyway?' she'd said. 'Is Art a thing that can be taught? Maybe today the student will become the teacher!' Her laugh at the end suggested that there was absolutely no way she thought we could teach her anything.

I looked at my watch. Ten minutes left. Was she ever going to stand up? Finally she put down the needles and roused herself.

'Time to share,' she called and started stalking round the room.

After a couple of trite patronising comments on Freya's pastel drawing she arrived in front of my desk. Standing Medusa-victim still, she stared at my sketch for a few seconds.

'Interesting,' she said. 'Mind if I share?' The familiar feeling of pride started to bubble up.

'This, class, is a perfect example of representative art.' My smile widened. *The new up-herself teacher had said 'perfect'.* 'See her technique, see how her lines exactly replicate the piece of ivy she's copying. It's almost photographic.' *I take it back. I like Ms Roberts. Ms Roberts is great!*

'Do you know what my lecturers at *Goldsmiths* said of representative art like this? "The lens has rendered it redundant."' *What?!* 'It is pointless! It looks like a photograph. So take a photograph. To reproduce exactly is to create nothing. This is not Art!' She flung my sketch down and my warm fuzzy feeling transformed into a boiling anger.

Her eyes flitted along the bench and alighted on Meena's piece.

'But this,' she cried, lifting it aloft like a lion cub about to be named by a particularly wise shaman-style baboon, 'is more like it! See the carefully abstracted leaves. They draw you in. *"Are they leaves or are they triangles?"* you ask. And the stalk. Or is it? It joins the leaves but it's the wrong colour, the wrong texture. It's closer to a piece of tangled barbed wire. It says: concentration camp. It says: refugee crisis. Inhumanity choking the world in the same way that ivy chokes a fence. And the colour – blue. Were you thinking in particular of refugees crossing the seas?'

'Yes, that's absolutely what I was going for,' Meena replied, completely deadpan.

'Your relatives, perhaps?'

'No, most of my relatives live round here.'

Ms Roberts ignored her, but flushed slightly pink.

'We will frame it immediately. Come class, come.'

Ms Roberts swept us into the corridor and stopped in front of one of my proudest creations. Self-portrait in charcoal. She removed it from the wall, opened the frame, tugged out my drawing, and replaced it with Meena's 'masterpiece'. There was a fire to her face as if she was a priest ordering the destruction of false idols.

'There. Regard. ART!' The paint hadn't quite dried so it smudged against the glass.

Mr Major had better get better soon. Maybe I'll ask Mum to send him a fruit basket. Suggest she puts some açai berries in it.

Art had dealt me such a blow that when I saw Lisa and April marching up after the lesson, no doubt to confront me about the message I'd left Ennis, I scuttled off and spent first break in the library. Anna came too and we helped Mrs Greenwood re-stack the returned books. It's worth doing this occasionally as:

(a) Mrs Greenwood is really nice;

(b) You get first dibs on any good books that come back; and

(c) Mrs Greenwood rewards all helpers with a custard cream, which just happens to be my favourite type of biscuit. Anna just eats them normally but I eat one side, scrape the cream off with my teeth and then eat the other side – a far more satisfying experience.

'Guess who was asking after you yesterday?' Anna asked mid-bite.

'I don't know, who?'

'I was at orchestra…'

'I don't need the back story.' Anna's rambles about the ups and downs and political intrigue of orchestra practice were always less than thrilling. All filler, no killer. And, anyway, I knew the 'who' in question had to be Rich Evans, but didn't want to look like I was bothered.

'Rich Evans!' cried Anna.

'OK.'

'I think he's really into you, India.'

'Right.'

'You should come to the Christmas Recital. He'll be

there. He'd be so pleased if you came. There's even going to be an audience participation bit at the end. Mr Hopper thought this might jazz things up a bit, get in a younger crowd.'

Christmas Recital. No one older than Year 7 would be seen dead at the Christmas Recital. Last year Anna even admitted that the audience age leapt from eleven to forty and most of the parents had been yawning if not asleep.

I didn't say anything, just paused. But it didn't come out as a normal pause at all. It came out as a pregnant pause. A big nine months' pregnant pause. I couldn't believe it, but part of me actually wanted to go to the recital. To hear Rich play. Chat with him afterwards.

Anna broke into my thoughts.

'You don't need to go out with Ennis, you know. Just because everyone else wants you to.'

'What if I want to? Have you ever thought of that, Anna? What if *I* want to?' I snapped at her and stormed off. I shouldn't have been so mean. I felt bad as soon as the words were coming out of my mouth, but I was just so fed up of everyone always telling me what I wanted or what I should do. Go out with Ennis. Don't go out with Ennis. Go out with Rich. Rich is a loser.

I had to take a stand. Make up my own mind. As if on cue, the lyrics to *Listen to Your Heart* popped into my head and burrowed itself a home. Thanks, Dad, for giving Mum *Roxette's* Greatest Hits CD for her last birthday. And it was all rubbish, the lyrics anyway. My heart was totally untrustworthy and flakey. My heart was as equally tempted by Ennis' long eyelashes and status as it was by Rich's kind goofiness. I had to ignore my heart. There was always something else you could do. I had to listen to my head.

Stay logical.

Make a list.

The bell was already ringing, but I ignored it and dashed into the toilets, pen and paper ready to tally up pros and cons.

*Ennis*
*Pros:*

- *Good-looking if you overlooked (ha ha) the height issue*
- *Sexy eyes*
- *Super cool*
- *Lisa and April would never look down on me and my friends again*

*Cons:*

- *A bit short*
- *Never really talked to him so he might be really stupid*

<u>Rich</u>
Pros:
- Really easy to talk to
- Still apparently interested even though he saw me close-up with horror-show make-up and even though my dad accused him of being a pervert

Cons:
- The opposite of cool
- Has a strangely high forehead
- A member of the orchestra
- Lisa and April would make my life hell for the rest of school

On paper everything became much clearer. You simply couldn't ignore a 2:4 con ratio. I had to try things with Ennis. Just because I hadn't ever really spoken to him didn't mean I couldn't speak to him or that we wouldn't get on. Just because he was cool didn't automatically mean he was stupid or unfunny or anything. And he had really sexy eyes and incredibly long eyelashes. I started picturing us turning up at all these events and him doing a squinty smile that showed off his eyelashes and saying, 'And this is my girlfriend, India Smythe,' and everyone else turning green with envy.

As I scuttled into double maths, I had a beaming smile on my face. Miss Owen's sarcastic comments about my being late just slid off me and I even turned round and met Lisa and April's eyes for the first time that day.

'Yes,' my super-confident face said. 'I'm ready to become one of you.'

My confidence started fading as lunch break approached. Lost in my Ennis-Rich, Rich-Ennis balancing, I realised I'd completely overlooked the fact that Ennis might well not be an option any more. *Hey … hi… hello.* He must have listened to my message by now and he hadn't called or messaged me back. When I'd turned my phone on there'd been a few texts on it from people who'd forgotten it'd been confiscated, but nothing from Ennis. Nada.

I tried to tell myself that everything would be OK. That I was just panicking due to low blood sugar levels. That lunch would sort everything out. The bell rang and we nabbed the end of a table by the door. Watching trays of chicken pie and peas, apple crumble and radioactively yellow custard walk past, I yet again regretted insisting on pack lunch at the start of the year. The trouble is you choose in September. In September sandwiches sound good. Soggy vegetables and custard so thick and sticky it can mend cracked pipes less so. It's amazing what a couple of months and a ten degree temperature drop can do to your tastebuds.

I sat in-between Anna and Meena and pulled my lunch items out my bag. Hmmmm. A cling film wrapped, hummus wholemeal roll, carrot sticks and an apple weren't going to give me that boost that I needed. Mum's into eating less meat at the moment so we never have anything good to make sandwiches with.

'Do you know how much methane cows produce, India?' Mum exploded when I last requested a burger.

'Probably less than Dad after a three bean curry,' I replied.

Cue eye rolls and a waterfall of condemnation, but someone had to say something. What if he's like that at work? Mum's been threatening to turn us all vegan for a month, but if that happened, Dad would probably lose his job and then we'd have to move house like Leila Bell. Or, worse still, he might get a temporary job as a teaching assistant at school. That's what happened with Rosie Gray's mum when she was made redundant. She helped out with Year 8 and her catchphrase was *nothing that can't be fixed with a smile and a hug*. Well, until she was told teachers couldn't hug kids any more. Rosie hasn't lived it down. Never will.

Meena, noticing my distress, gave me half her Monster Munch. Truly delicious. 'Chemical puffs' Mum calls them, dismissively. 'Devil's food.' I don't care which malevolent forces have been involved in devising the flavouring combinations. I don't even think they're any worse for you than other types of crisps. They're just totally, utterly delicious. Monster Munch rocks.

Fifteen minutes later and Lisa and April shimmied over as I'd taken my first, admittedly oversized, bite of apple.

'We're going to the Fence now. Are you coming?' Lisa asked, staring in distaste at my distended hamster cheek.

It was happening. It was really happening. I was being invited to the Fence by the coolest girls in our year. I could feel the respect radiating off Meena.

'Um… (*desperate swallow, followed by classy semi-choke cough*) … yes, yes I am.' Time to confront this thing head-on. At least this way I'd find out for certain if Ennis was still interested. 'Fears are there to be faced' is one of Dad's favourite sayings, although, thinking about it, he always lets the phone ring out if he's expecting a stressful call and has been known to fake flu before a major presentation.

April interrogated me as we walked.

'So, I'm taking it you've organised a date now?'

'Er. Well. Not exactly.'

'But you've messaged him?' Anxiety-stained anger was starting to creep into her voice.

'I … I left him a message.'

'You what?' April's eyes were slits of flashing steel. She stopped in the middle of the grass. Halfway to the Fence. 'What did you say – word for word? Has he called you back?'

*Hey … hi … hello*

'I, I don't remember exactly, but no, he hasn't called back yet.'

'I told you she's a liability,' hissed Lisa. 'We can't take her with us to the Fence. We have to leave her here.'

'No. Damn it, they're already there and we've been seen,' April snapped back. 'Keep walking, it'd be weirder to bin her midway. And smile. Not like that, India, for God's sake. They don't need to be able to count your teeth.'

'If you've messed this up, India…' Lisa threatened.

'I hope I haven't. I'm so sorry if I have,' I stammered, breathing a bit heavily from all the stress.

April recoiled.

'Oh my God, have you been eating Monster Munch? We're on our way to talk to Ennis and Anthony and you've been eating Monster Munch!?!'

'Errrr.' There was nothing to say. There was no point

denying it, and anyway, my fingers were still stained slightly orange, which was a bit of a giveaway. It hadn't crossed my mind that my breath might be an issue. I was a moron. I wasn't cut out for this. I'd just have to try and breathe in as I spoke, to stop any more pickled onion particles leaving my mouth.

Lisa and April's walk got even bendier and swayier than normal as we took the final steps up to the Fence.

'Hey girls.' Anthony greeted us with a grin and intertwined fingers with April, before giving her a full-on snog through a wire diamond. There was no forehead butting fence moment, no awkward lips misjudging the gap and closing round green plastic covered wire instead. They were unbelievably good at this. My brain started trying to calculate whether there was any way they could have hit the ten thousand hour practice mark. Twenty minutes at first break, followed by a potential hour at lunchtime times five days a week…

'India.' Ennis winked at me and smiled.

'Ennis.' I smiled back, considering attempting a wink of my own, but then abandoning it, which I think was a good call. Although, judging from Ennis's slightly weirded-out expression, there's a good chance the muscles around my eye and upper cheek did the first tiny preparatory muscle squeeze so I could have looked like someone having a mini stroke.

'Got your message,' he continued.

'I'm so sorry about that,' interrupted Lisa. 'We didn't know.'

'What?' laughed Ennis. 'It was cool. Ironic, yeah?'

'Oh yeah, totally,' I laughed back.

'I mean an answerphone message!?!'

'Totally!' I hadn't realised how hard it would be sounding all chipper whilst not exhaling Monster Munch breath. Or that I was apparently now someone who said 'totally' a lot.

'Oh yeah,' tinkled Lisa, joined by April, who'd come up for air.

'Nice touch leaving out your number,' he said, winking again. To be honest, he winks a bit too much, but then again maybe anyone would if they had eyelashes as long as that.

'Well, that's why they call me Little Miss Nice Touch,' I replied.

A beat, and then everyone, including me, registered what I'd just said. Lisa and April's mouths hit the floor and Ennis started roaring with laughter while I flushed scarlet. *Little Miss Nice Touch?! When I'm not at school solving quadratic equations, I'm offering illicit services down dimly lit alleys. Who am I? – Yes, Little Miss Nice Touch?!?!!*

'Really? Well I hope I get to find out more about that,' Ennis said between 'Ha's'.

Great, so now he thinks I'm easy as well as a moron.

'You're really the funniest, India. I can see why you guys hang around with her.'

'Oh she is,' Lisa simpered. 'Just hysterical.'

'So ... how about Friday night?' Ennis said. To me. This was it. Ennis was asking me out. To my face.

'Sure. Yes. That sounds fine. I mean good. Yes.'

'I'll pick you up at eight.'

*Pick me up.*

*As in come to my house.*

*As in highly likely to meet my parents.*

'Can't I, like, meet you somewhere?'

'India,' April's voice was a low warning growl. 'He said he'd pick you up, OK. Ennis and Anthony are *gentlemen.*'

'Yeah, India, it's their thing,' Lisa chimed in reproachfully. To her, my lack of knowledge of Ennis's assumed qualities was equivalent to not knowing London was the capital of England. Or that mascara darkened and lengthened eye lashes. But it wasn't fair. Why couldn't my thing be not liking boys coming anywhere near my house?

'Just message me your address or something.'

'I can only text on my phone.'

'OK. Keeping it old school. Like it.'

The bells on both sides of the Fence started to ring.

'Laterz,' grinned Ennis, before turning and walking away.

'Laterz!' I called after him before Lisa could hush me.

'Only one person ever says "Laterz"', she hissed. 'You don't repeat Laterz.'

'Sorry,' I mumbled, spinning round to look at Ennis's retreating figure. He didn't look back. In the distance someone was hotfooting it across the grass with big curls and a cello on his back. I wondered if it was Rich Evans.

'And never look back. Once you turn away from the Fence you only look forwards.'

So I banished all thoughts of calling out to potential Rich. Or even of looking in that direction any further. Instead I turned my eyes towards St Mary's and kept on walking.

The rules.

If this was supposed to be fun, why did there have to be so many rules?!

Friday night.

I'd cleared it with Mum that I could go out. My grounding technically only finished at midnight but Mum seemed to appreciate that I'd made an effort this week – I hadn't been late for school, I'd been helpful around the house: kept my bag to the edge of the hall, hung my coat up, correctly angled the milk in the fridge. I hadn't told her exactly what I'd be doing, just said something like, 'Is it OK if I go out on Friday night?' so she doubtless assumed I'd be watching films or eating pizza at Meena or Anna's.

'Do you want food before you go out?' was her only question.

Did I want food? Was I going to be eating with Ennis? I had no idea what we were going to be doing. I hadn't asked in case that was another thing I was just supposed to know. Another unwritten rule. *A date past seven-thirty on a Friday night invariably includes a burger.* Or something like that.

'India, *food*?'

*What to do, what to do?*

'There's some three bean casserole left in the fridge that I could heat up.'

Decision made.

I hung around in my room till just before eight. Trying on various outfits. Experimenting with subtle make-up. Attempting a soft wax/hairspray combo as a preventative anti-frizz bouffant manoeuvre. Trying not to hyperventilate. My brain was scrambling so I texted the gang for advice.

'Something low cut and brightly coloured,' from Meena. 'But only if your push-up bra is clean.'

'Something warm,' from Anna. 'It's going to be cold tonight.'

Great, thanks guys. So, put that together and you get a low-cut, fluorescent yellow duffel coat. No problem, I'll just pull that out my wardrobe.

In the end I went with jeans, silver-grey lacy top, a bit of mascara and dark-red lip gloss. I tried out different bras and decided on my grey one. It wasn't push-up and didn't give me a great silhouette or anything, but it was the least noticeable under my top and the straps always stayed in place and didn't dig into my shoulders. Finishing touch was a quick spritz of perfume. *Lucky* by *Natalia*. Aunty Hope gave it to me last Christmas and Mum did a huffy little shoulder shrug as I unwrapped it. 'Totally inappropriate,' she'd sniffed. Just because Aunty Hope is a lot cooler than her and has aged quite a lot better even though she's two years older. OK, both of them have completely dyed hair, but Aunty Hope's looks a lot less dyed than Mum's. More brown. Less orange. First I dabbed the perfume behind my ears and on the sides of my neck, but that seemed to lack a sense of occasion. Of drama. After all, tonight I wasn't India Smythe, prolific eater of pizza and watcher of Netflix. Tonight I was Date of Ennis, envy of every girl in Year

10. This called for pizzazz, which, come to think of it, actually does sound a lot like pizza.

I did the whole spray-loads-of-perfume-out-in-front-of-you-and-then-strut-through-the-cloud thing. Looking back on it, I'm not sure if this is just a thing that only men do normally, but, if so, women need to get in on the act. It's really fun. And, as a bonus, I felt mature. Powerful. So I kept spraying and strutting. Tonight had to go well. I figured I might as well be as *Lucky* as possible.

At 8:00pm I took a deep breath, twisted the door handle and padded downstairs. The plan was to watch out from behind the living room curtains. As soon as I saw a figure step onto the front path, I'd be off, out the door, without so much as a glance back.

Dad wasn't home yet. He was 'catching up with some of his old band friends' so I just had to get past Mum. It was one-on-one.

'India, you look nice.' Damn. Mum was sat on the living room couch watching TV. In active wear. Cuddling a hot-water bottle as defence against the thermostat. At least she had one of her longer jumpers on. Her tone was surprised, not suspicious. I had to keep it that way.

'Um, thanks. Just thought I'd dress up a bit, you know.'

'So, where exactly are you going?'

'Er… We're not quite sure yet.'

'But it'll be Meena's or Anna's, right?' Suspicion had now officially entered the room.

BRINGGGGGGG!!

Saved by the bell. Well no. Probably the opposite of that. But, either way, the bell was ringing.

'I'll get it,' I said, dashing for the door, grabbing my coat and pale pink scarf (strategically left at the end of the banister) on the way.

I'd hoped Mum would stay in the living room and I could slip out with a mumbled goodbye, my evening plans left ambiguous.

'If it's one of those door-to-door sellers claiming to be just out of prison, say no and shut the door, India. Those oven gloves I got last month were terrible quality. So thin. I burnt my hand on the butternut squash lasagna, remember?'

I wasn't really listening. I had the front door fractionally open and was peering round the gap, fixed smile on face, 'Here's Johnny' style.

My heart did a little flip. There, on my doorstep, stood Ennis. He was all smart. He'd dressed up. For *me*. Nice jeans and this cool dark blue coat that brought out his eyes. Nike air trainers giving him a bit of a height boost. He was smiling, showing exactly the right amount of teeth. I tried to concentrate. Take it all in so I could relay every single detail to Meena and Anna later.

'Hey India. Is everything OK?' Ennis looked a bit weirded out, so I opened the door slightly wider so he could see I still had a body and tried to relax my face. My concentration face can be a bit off-putting. Meena was the first to point this out to me and I didn't believe her until I checked by staring in a mirror while I tried to work out the first ten cubic numbers. By 216 I had to turn away; it was so horrific.

'India! India – what's going on?' Mum had left the living room.

'I'll just be a sec,' I whispered to Ennis.

'Why are you whispering?'

Before I could answer, Mum was right behind me, hand on the door.

'Who is it, India?'

'It's … it's Ennis, Mum.'

The air started to crackle with static. Mum's hand wrapped round the edge of the door.

'India, a word. Excuse us, … ENNIS,' and she shut the door in Ennis's face. Mum shut the door in Ennis's face!

'India, what's going on?' Her tone was ice.

'I'm going on a date with Ennis,' I answered quietly. 'He's at St Joseph's. Mum, please open the door.'

'Ennis who?'

'I don't understand.'

'What's his surname? This Ennis must have a surname, mustn't he? I'm not going to let my daughter wander off for the evening with a strange young man when I don't even know his surname! What sort of mother do you take me for?!'

I wracked my brain. Nothing. Zero. I didn't have a clue what his surname was. He was Ennis. Of Anthony and Ennis. They were like Ant and Dec. They didn't need surnames.

'I don't know his surname,' I hissed back. I should have lied. I should have made something up. It would have been so easy. *Carter, Jones, Thompson*. There're so many believable bland surnames out there. Or I could have thrown caution to the wind and gone exotic. *Zebedee*. She'd never imagine that I'd make up a Zebedee. But I didn't. I said nothing. Just stood there, opening and closing my mouth like a dumb goldfish. I think the stress of the situation must have been killing my brain cells.

'Well, go and ask him then.' Mum's hands were on her hips now. That was bad. She normally keeps her hands well away from her hips as she thinks she's got a big butt and doesn't like to draw attention to that area – as if hands rather than leggings were the problem. Once her hands are on her hips, you've had it. There's no changing her mind.

I slowly opened the door. Ennis was still stood there, now looking pretty freaked out.

'Well?' Mum's voice, a cattle prod behind me.

'Um, Ennis… What's your surname?'

'What? Barratt, why?' The smile had completely gone from his face.

'Just a minute.'

I was back on the other side of the door.

'Mum, it's Barratt. I'm going out with Ennis Barratt.'

'Fine.' Mum threw the door open.

'Good evening Ennis Barratt,' Mum said, completely immune to the supposedly charming grin Ennis aimed in her direction. 'Make sure India's back by ten-thirty. I'll need your number in case I can't get hold of my daughter.' Mum headed over to the hall table. I expected her to fetch the pad of paper and pen that always sat there, but she didn't. She picked up her phone instead and opened up the contacts page. 'Is that Barratt with one "t" or two?'

'Er, two.'

Pause. Horrible, horrible pause.

'There we go. New contact: Ennis Barratt with two ts. And your number?'

Ennis reeled off a string of numerals in monotone while I begged the earth to swallow me whole. Mum had just added Ennis to her list of contacts. There was no way this evening could get any worse.

The number entered and Mum finally silent, we turned to leave.

'Mums normally dig me,' Ennis muttered as we headed down the path. 'That … that's never happened before.'

We turned left down my street and then headed right onto Willow Road. I didn't know where we were going, I just kind of let Ennis guide me. I think I was still too stunned to speak. I wrapped my scarf round my neck and pulled my coat tightly round me, already regretting the choice of the thin black wool one instead of the thick green parka that's basically a duvet with arms. Ennis was clearly weirded out too. He was so tense that his legs weren't bending properly at the knee, so he sort of goose-stepped along the pavement.

Four streets later my vocal chords returned.

'So…' I tried to make my voice sound light. Sexy. Adopted. Free from any trace of Mum's psycho DNA. 'Where are we going?'

'You'll see,' Ennis replied mysteriously, and winked. The lack of information was slightly annoying, but I was grateful at least for the wink. A sign that he was recovering, snapping out of shock.

'Come here,' he continued, 'it's cold,' and in one smooth move, he'd wrapped his arm round my shoulders.

I'd always felt a bit envious when I'd seen other couples walking round, the guy's arm around the girl's shoulders. The ultimate gesture of protection. Anna says it irritates her when couples are like that. That it's like the guys are claiming ownership. Me caveman … grunt … this my woman … grunt. But I don't agree. When you see guys with their hand round the back of a girl's neck, now that's freaky controlling, but an arm round their shoulders – well, I think it's romantic. What I hadn't realised, however, was that you need a certain height differential for it to work properly. And Ennis just wasn't quite tall enough, even with his Nike Airs, or I was too tall. However you looked at it, the result was the same i.e. that his right shoulder, the one doing the wrapping, was jerked up out of its joint at a weird, semi-hunchbacked angle and then too much of his body weight was falling, via his lower arm, onto my shoulders. It was like walking carrying a boulder. Or how your arm feels when you sleep on it all night so all the blood leaves it and you wake up to this massively heavy limb over which your brain seems to have no control.

Anyway, I glanced at Ennis to check if he was

enjoying this any more than I was and he caught my eye and shot me a strained smile in return. Great, so he was clearly equally uncomfortable, but wasn't going to say anything either. We were going to pretend this was great. Totally great.

More silence.

'You smell good,' he offered.

'Thanks,' I replied.

And that was it for conversation. Neither of us saying anything more. Silence punctuated with car noises and footsteps. And it was awkward. Really awkward. I tried to think of topics of conversation, things I'd talk about with Meena and Anna if they were here instead of Ennis – *Riverdale*, school, the fact that the driver of the red car parking up in front of us looked crazily like Cheryl Blossom – but nothing seemed good enough. Cool enough.

Then I started panicking about what we were going to do. We were clearly heading to the town centre. Ennis was the same year as me, but whereas I'm born at the start of August so the baby of the year and destined to have smaller boobs than everyone else forever, he's a late September kid so one of the oldest. (Meena told me while trying to work out our star sign compatibility. Apparently it's four out of five hearts; our distinct personalities balancing the other's out, helped along by the fact that our signs are 'sextile' which apparently means two signs apart. It took Meena over two minutes of choke splutter laughing before she managed to share the 'sextile' definition. She's so immature sometimes. Although it was pretty funny.) Anyway, all this meant that Ennis had already turned fifteen. OK, he was quite short, but short didn't make you look young. He probably looked seventeen or eighteen. What if he wanted to go to a pub? What if he had some convincing fake ID and wanted to go to a pub and I got us thrown out immediately for being blatantly underage?

My heart rate increased.

*BOOM BOOM BOOM.*

Or, or, what if he wanted to go to the cinema and watch some really scary, gory film and I didn't get let in? Or… I did get in and was sick? Sick all over him? I can't see any form of blood in reality or on screen without feeling instantly nauseous. It doesn't even have to be a horror or serial killer murder. I once threw up at Meena's when she was flicking through the channels and stopped for a few seconds on a documentary about NHS surgeons.

*BREATHE. BREATHE.*

*Be at one with the moment.*

*Achieve mental clarity and possible enlightenment.*

*Focus on the facts.*

Ennis had a backpack on. Why would he have a backpack on if we were going to the pub or to the cinema? Guys didn't generally bring bags. They didn't take spare clothes in case they got cold; they just froze and got grumpy. They didn't need access to emergency make-up. The bag must have a purpose. Maybe he'd planned something really good. My brain started to race. Everyone went on about Ennis being a gentleman. That that was his *thing*. Gentlemen were romantic, right? Gentlemanliness and romance surely went hand in hand. So maybe he'd planned this big romantic evening. Maybe we were going to have a moonlit picnic? Or go on a night-time adventure ... a treasure hunt with clues? I've always thought the most romantic thing ever would be running around softly lit streets on a quest with some guy. Solving problems together. Laughing and holding hands.

'Nearly there,' Ennis declared as we turned left onto the High Street. We were right by The Stag. Ennis slowed down as we passed the first window.

*BOOM, BOOM, BOOM.*

*NO, NO, NO!!!!!!*

But then he speeded up again and I realised he'd just paused to check out his reflection in the glass.

'This way.' He ducked down the alley straight after the pub. Me and Meena never use it. It's very narrow and badly lit so you feel like you're walking into a crime report. Might as well bring your own roll of police tape with you. It's the sort of place Little Miss Nice Touch might hang out.

'You sure about this?' I asked Ennis.

'What? 'Course. It's the quickest way. Don't worry – I'll protect you.' And another wink.

Ennis had to unhook his arm from my shoulders so we could walk single file. I think that's the main reason he chose the route. Seconds later and we were on the Green. The same place I'd been with Yan. The same place Sammy Bevan had been with Pete Driver. And I'd thought Ennis was cool. Special. A *gentleman*. Do guys do nothing nowadays but take girls to greens? I should have worn my bloody parka.

'Don't you love this place?' he said, doing a sweeping motion with his arm, like he was showing me a hidden beach or secret glade deep in the forest. Rather than a twenty metre by twenty metre square of patchy grass fringed by benches – home of tramps and the local dog toilet. What was there to say?

'Um, yes, sure. *Love* it,' I replied.

'Let's sit over there. By the *plane* trees. It's so romantic.' I swear there was a slight inflection in his voice on the word 'plane' as if he was wanting extra points for plant identification. Like the peeling, mottled trunk didn't make it one of the easiest trees out there to identify. The horticultural equivalent of a pigeon. It would have been different if it was something rarer. A Japanese maple, perhaps. I wouldn't mind having a Japanese maple pointed out to me.

I forced my face to smile again.

Ennis took my hand and walked me over to the foot of the group of trees on the other side. I squatted, putting my hand down to feel the grass. It was wet. Brilliant. This night just got better and better. I thought about giving up and going home, but then I pictured the consequences. The fallout.

| | |
|---|---|
| Lisa and April: | *You loser, India, you've made us look bad, no one makes us look bad.* |
| Meena: | *This is ENNIS, India, ENNIS; you have to give him a chance.* |
| Mum: | *Why are you back so early? What happened? What did he do? Well I'll just call him myself if you don't tell me … open Contacts…* |

I shut out the sea of imaginary, angry female faces and forced myself to sit. Ennis dived after me and yanked me back up again.

'What are you doing, India? I didn't bring you here

to make you sit on the grass!" He sounded put out. Like I'd insulted him.

'Here.' He took off his backpack and opened up the drawstring section, pulling out a checked, plastic-backed picnic rug.

I didn't have to fake a smile this time.

A moonlit picnic! To think I'd been about to leave! I was going to have the second most romantic evening possible. Unless of course, deeper in the bag there was also a map and some clues tucked away too. Then we'd have hit the bull's eye! I tried not to get my hopes up too much.

'Oh, wow!' I murmured, 'Thanks!'

Ennis smiled. Ego restored.

'Have a seat, my lady.' His eyes crinkled up as he smiled and he batted his long lashes. I take it back. This was going to be a great night. What had he brought for us to eat? I'd kill for some cheese sandwiches. Or cold pizza. Or any flavour crisps.

My mouth started to salivate and I think I might have even licked my lips as Ennis looked at me quizzically before saying, 'You've eaten, haven't you?'

Just a rug.

No food.

There was no food!

'Eaten? Yes, of course.' I nodded enthusiastically. Like

I'd just consumed a feast. An all-you-can-eat buffet of epic proportions. Rather than the truth. That I was so hungry I was beginning to reabsorb my own intestine, like a bar-tailed godwit at the end of a seven thousand mile migratory flight. (Dad got the Bill Bailey bird-watching book for Christmas last year. It was surprisingly interesting.)

I sat down next to Ennis. Rather cold. And not able to see very much. The moon was a cross section through a contact lens and the nearest streetlamp was ten metres away and only flickered on and off occasionally. Like it might be communicating with us from the Upside Down.

'So, this is nice,' I said lamely. I snuck a look at my watch, pressing the light button. My trusty Casio. Waterproof, shockproof, reliable: a birthday present from Anna. 8:14pm. I'd stay till ten. That was one hour and forty-six minutes. Allow ten minutes to get home. I had to survive the next one hour and thirty-six minutes.

'I nearly forgot,' Ennis exclaimed, reaching into his pocket. 'Got to record the moment. You look so hot on camera.'

He flipped his phone onto selfie mode. Damn. Damn. Damn. There's a reason massively famous photographers don't just march models into the dark and then flash a torch in their face. And this time I didn't have centimetre-thick make-up on. This was not going to go well, but what could I do? I swivelled my head to my good side and tried to look alluring.

Ennis's finger hit the button.

Oh. No.

Terrible.

I looked like a vampire bride. Bleached out face, dark eyes, and a weird smile. Alluring is not a good look for me. Ennis looked pretty rough too. The flash had given him pink, puffy eyes. He visibly flinched before turning his phone onto torch mode and semi-chucking it to the other end of the rug.

'Maybe it's best sometimes to keep stuff private, you know? Just for you and me.' I nodded my agreement. 'Anyway, this way it'll give us some atmosphere, you know, like candles.'

The phone light was harsh and white. It was like we were in a dimly lit public toilet. I can't quite imagine Mum using it at a dinner party:

Dad:   *Shall I put some candles on the table?*

Mum:  *No, don't bother. We'll just stick a couple of phones on torch mode in the middle instead. It'll give exactly the same atmosphere.*

'So?' I asked. 'What now?'

Ennis acted like he hadn't heard, instead swivelling his head slightly so that he was now staring up at me through his eyelash hedge. Maybe he's got a good side too.

'You looked really hot at my party,' Ennis murmured, stroking my hair with his left hand. 'You're so pretty. And funny. And sweet. I can see why April and Lisa hang out with you.'

OK, I'd like to say that the fact that he'd started murmuring compliments at me made no difference whatsoever. That I'd read enough Aesop's fables in my youth to know better. The fox that pretends to befriend the chicken and then gobbles it up. And to be able to say that my attention was still focused on the cold and the fact that his vowel sounds swung weirdly between South London and posh. But sadly, embarrassingly, that would be rubbish. I am weak. I am flesh. And there was something about having one of the two coolest guys at St Joseph's stroking *my* hair and calling *me* pretty that suddenly meant that it was A-OK that I was lying, unfed and freezing on a square of plastic on the Green on a foggy November evening.

'I love... mumblemumblemumble,' he whispered.

'Sorry, what was that?' I whispered back, leaning in.

'I said I love running my hand through your hair,' he whispered again, his mouth now only centimetres from mine.

I smiled. And fluttered my eyelashes. Deep down I knew he was lying. I've felt Mum's hair after she's sprayed it with Maximum Lift and Hold and it's like stroking a broom. Or a straw helmet. But he said it so smoothly. And his eyelashes were so beautifully long. And his breath smelt like spearmint.

He was gazing into my face, waiting. What did he want? Oh, probably a compliment in return. God, I'm terrible at this.

'You... Er...'

'Yes?'

*He knows he has nice eyes. Surprise him. Choose something else. Anything else.*

'Um, you have ... nice teeth.'

He laughed. Laughed like I'd made the greatest joke ever.

'I think I'm going to have to kiss you now, India.'

He closed his eyes.

I closed my eyes.

This was it.

Ennis of Anthony and Ennis was going to kiss me. If social life was scored, this was the equivalent of a bonus fifty points for putting all your letters down at the same time in Scrabble.

His lips bumped and squashed into mine and immediately his tongue was poking into my mouth. I wasn't expecting this. Not immediately, so first his tongue hit my teeth then his teeth hit my teeth, which jarred and sent this weird tremor of shock round my mouth, like if you eat ice cream when you've got a cold.

'Relax, India,' he murmured.

And the tongue was back.

He had moves, that's for sure. (I know he's kissed a lot of girls. For real. Not like one of those guys who claims to have kissed loads of girls, but you know it's rubbish and every girl implicated explodes in indignant, furious denial. I know Ennis has kissed lots of girls because I've heard lots of girls say it. He was a status symbol. If you kissed Ennis you didn't exactly keep it quiet.) His tongue was everywhere. Poking, rolling, the odd lip chew, and I tried to keep up. It was like mouth gym. And it felt good … quite good. Not fireworks good, though, but maybe there's no such thing as fireworks. There weren't fireworks with Yan. Maybe snogging is just quite nice. Full stop. And all the books and films that say otherwise have the equivalent truth quotient of all the books and films about inspiring bad-ass teachers who turn around failing schools through the power of rap.

Ennis came up for air and kept his eyes all squinty half closed. Like they could only open a crack. I did the same. I was slowly learning the rules. Squinty half-closed eyes must be sexy.

'Are you, OK?' he breathed.

'Yeeesssss,' I breathed back, channelling sex kitten.

'It's just that your eyes have gone all squinty,' the breathiness had gone.

'So have yours.'

'Oh, OK then.'

A beat. And then…

'You have such a sexy neck, India. It's such a shame to cover it up.' And heavy breathing man was back. Very slowly, he unwound my scarf and then let it fall to the ground before dipping his head and starting to kiss my neck. From just below my jaw bone and down my jugular. There's got to be better, more appropriate vocab to describe this. More sensual. I doubt *Fifty Shades* was full of jaw bones and jugulars. I'll have to ask Mum. Yeah right.

But the important thing is this felt better. Pretty amazing actually. His lips traced and nibbled up and down and then stayed in one place. Gently sucking.

I wasn't quite sure what I was supposed to be doing so I just sort of stroked his back and arms a bit and made some 'Mmmmm' noises while at the same time wondering whether he was enjoying this too or whether I should take over and start kissing his neck and hoping that I didn't misjudge it and go actual all-out vampire on him.

His breathing was getting heavier and heavier. A good sign surely. He must have been into it.

'India,' he began mumbling. 'India, I can't breathe.'

Ha! I thought. And I was worried about my performance. Turns out I'm so sexy, guys can't breathe around me.

'Seriously, India, *GASP, GASP*, I can't breathe.'

Ennis detached himself from my throat and I shone the phone light at his face.

Dear God.

His eyes were now completely bloodshot, puffed out like golf balls and only open in a two millimetre slit. His lips too were swollen. Bee-stung. Like some horrific Real Beverly Hills Wife post-tenth collagen injection. Around his lips were lots of red lumps. Smaller than mosquito bites. But pretty similar to the cluster of flea bites I got round my left knee last year after Rebus had slept on my bed. He looked like 'infected person three' on a poster I once made on the Plague. Had Ennis caught the Plague? Which would mean – I've now got the Plague!!!!!!

Must keep calm. Like a nurse in one of those cool starched blue uniforms. A stethoscope round my neck. Chart in hand. Maybe I should become a nurse. I took another dispassionate, diagnostic look at Ennis's face.

'Oh, God, Oh, God! What's wrong with you?' I

blurted out. 'Agggghhhhh!!!!' Cross off nurse from potential careers list.

Ennis was clutching at his throat. Focus. What was that acronym we'd done at school? DR something. DR what? Hmmmmm. DR ABC that's it. Now what do the letters stand for?

'Call an ambulance!' Ennis spluttered.

Yes. Yes, that's what I needed to do.

With shaky hands I punched in the numbers.

The operator answered immediately. Calm. Professional.

'Ambulance!' I garbled. 'We need an ambulance. My...' how to describe him? 'Boyfriend' was too forward but 'friend' maybe too platonic ... hmmm... 'My... Ennis can't breathe...'

The ambulance arrived within three minutes. Which is pretty amazing if you think about it. Take that, people who constantly moan about the NHS! It pulled up on the pavement at the edge of the Green, blue lights flashing, and two paramedics leapt out and rushed over.

They took one look at Ennis and marched him up the ramp into the back of the ambulance and stuck a gas mask over his mouth. The male paramedic talked to him calmly, explaining what they were doing, while the female one actually pumped the adrenalin gas into the mask and administered steroids to widen his throat again.

'What do you think it is?' I asked quietly when they'd finished and Ennis's breathing had normalised.

'An allergic reaction, most likely,' the female one, Abeer, replied. Maybe they took it in turns speaking so that neither of them lost their voice. It was probably a long shift. She turned to Ennis.

'Do you have any known allergies?'

Ennis shook his head.

'The worst reaction is around your mouth. Have you eaten anything different?'

Head shake again. My stomach rumbled as evidence.

'Drunk anything? Taken anything?'

Double head shake.

What the hell had happened then?

Abeer didn't say anything for a few seconds, her eyes lingering on his face and then on my neck.

'What about perfume?' she said eventually.

'Um, I'm not sure.'

Oh double triple no.

*Lucky.*

I'd practically swum through a river of *Lucky* and then he'd basically sucked it off my neck. It was my fault. All my fault. I'd almost killed Ennis. I was an attempted murderer! I started to breathe really quickly. Any minute now, it'd be my turn on the adrenaline mask.

'Do you normally use hypoallergenic bath and shower products?' Abeer was not letting this one go.

'No. Lynx mostly.'

My breathing normalised a bit. Surely if your body can handle Lynx it could handle pretty much anything. Unless... Unless there was something specific in *Lucky*. I hadn't seen it anywhere in the shops. It wasn't exactly advertised on billboards. At least Ennis didn't seem to be connecting the dots. The link between his saying I smelt nice, kissing my neck then swelling up like the elephant man not forming in his brain.

'Hmmm. Well, we're going to take you into hospital for observation. Mike, call ahead, will you?'

'Um, shall I stay?' I asked quietly, not quite knowing what my role was here. The protocol. Was it family members only? Potential allergens to travel separately?

'Stay, please,' Ennis squeezed my hand and I sat down next to him. 'And ... er maybe put your scarf on, so you ... don't get cold.'

Mike passed me my scarf with a smirk. Which was a bit rude, I thought. OK so he zoomed round all night saving countless lives, but did that really give him the right to go round laughing at young love?!

Phoning ahead is amazing. We didn't even need to fill out any forms; we were just whizzed through onto a ward and deposited in one of the curtained-off sections while people checked Ennis's heart rate, blood pressure and so on. The new nurse went through the same list of questions and I felt myself getting hotter and hotter, knowing we were just a couple of head shakes away from someone mentioning PERFUME again. I unwrapped my scarf and took off my coat. I needed some air.

'I'm just going to go and get a snack,' I said. *And wash off some perfume.* 'Do you want anything?'

'Nah, I'm fine thanks.'

I headed towards the vending machine, slotted in one pound fifty and retrieved a grab bag of Monster Munch. My stomach growled a thank you. I then skirted the edge of the nurses' bay, found myself on the receiving end of a few sniggers (so – it's a grab bag of Monster Munch – yes, I'm going to eat ALL of it, but it's my only dinner and I'm not exactly obese – stop judging me, haters) and managed to find an unoccupied loo.

Locking the door behind me, I pumped soap into my hands, foamed it up and faced myself in the mirror, ready to wash away the evidence. Cleanse the neck of poison. Neck… Oh my God, my NECK!

Two dark red circles, already heading their way down the colour chart to black, stared back at me. Like eyes on a smiley face. No wonder everyone had been smirking and sniggering at me. I was a joke. Ennis had given me love bites. LOVE BITES! Like the tackiest thing ever!!! Agghhhh!!! *I'd* been monster munched!!!! How was I going to deal with this?! How was I going to cover it up?! What would Mum say?! What would Dad say?!!!!!!

Mum.

Dad.

The two words hovered above me like thunder clouds. What was the time? In the stress of everything I'd totally forgotten about the time.

*Trusty Casio on my wrist, who art the most screwed girl in all the kingdom? You are, India Smythe.*

It was ten forty-five. Fifteen minutes past curfew. Hell. Hell. Hell. This was bad. Properly bad. I wanted to curl up in a ball and never leave the loo ever again. I'd be found in fifty years' time, a desiccated corpse, like one of the Pompeii victims, but harder to explain. I couldn't even text. I'd left my phone in my coat pocket.

There was a knock on the door.

'Is someone in there?'

Was there no privacy?!!! What exactly was the rush???? How ridiculous!!

'We need to take an urgent urine sample!'

OK, maybe not so ridiculous.

I opened the door and, shoulders hunched up to my ears to shield horrific neck bites from view, I scuttled back to Ennis's section.

'Where've you been?' he asked.

'Not now,' I snapped. 'My neck. What did you do to my neck?!'

'Sorry. Thought you were into it. I kind of got carried away.'

'Hmmppphh!'

'Most girls don't mind.'

'Pahhhhhh!' Seems I had lost the power of speech and was reduced to just making weird exploding noises.

'Also, India. I think your mum's a bit mad. She's started texting me. The last one wasn't very nice.'

Damn. I had to shut this down. I reached for my coat and pulled my phone out from the pocket. It was on silent. There were twenty-three missed calls. There was nothing to do but bite the bullet.

I called home. Mum picked up after a single ring and then exploded into my ear.

'India... Where the hell are you? I was worried sick... Rah rah rah!!!!!!' Maybe the noises are genetic.

'Mum, I'm at the hospital.'

Silence.

'India,' her voice had dropped about twenty decibels and all the anger was gone. I'd never heard her sound so scared. 'Are you OK?' The guilt was a sucker punch.

'Yes, Mum. I'm fine. Please don't worry. I'm so sorry I didn't call. Ennis had an allergic reaction … to something he ate … and I had to call an ambulance and get him to hospital. I didn't realise how late it was. It was all such a shock.'

'That's OK love. That's a lot to deal with. How's he doing?'

Mum was being understanding. Mum was being OK. Which made me feel like the world's worst daughter.

'He's fine now.'

'Can I come and pick you up?'

I looked at Ennis. 'Is it OK if my mum picks me up now?'

'Sure. My Dad's coming in about fifteen minutes anyway.'

'Now's great, Mum, thanks.'

'I'm on my way… Oh, and India,' Mum added, 'please apologise to Ennis for my last couple of texts. I may have used some rather inappropriate language.'

The weekend was an exercise in subterfuge. I'm adding spy to my list of potential careers as I think I'm pretty good at it. There's some space now I've crossed off nursing.

I woke up crazily early on Saturday morning with a weird face sweat – well it seemed weird until I realised that I still had my wool scarf triple-wrapped round my neck. I'd been so worried that Mum and Dad would see the love bites that I hadn't risked taking it off downstairs when we got in and then I was paranoid that they'd come and wake me up in the morning before I could conceal the evidence.

To be fair, Dad never wakes me up. He never comes into my room full stop. He sees it as a no-go zone as he's so scared that he might accidentally stumble across me getting changed.

Mum's a different matter though. At weekends she always marches in with a cup of tea at around eight. It's really annoying as the tea is an objectively 'kind' gesture so I can't have a go – *sorry, India, so sorry I brought you a nice cup of hot tea, I'm such a TERRIBLE mother* – but I know that she uses it as a weapon to get me out of bed so it's actually really manipulative. Anyway, I couldn't risk her coming in, seeing that Ennis had gone all Dracula on me and then dropping the tea in a screaming fit.

But one major advantage of the 6am face sweat wake-up was that I had two hours to experiment with different cover-up methods. Two hours in which to avert Armageddon.

First Attempt: Concealer. You'd have thought that if concealer can get rid of dark circles under your eyes it could deal with a couple of dark circle bruises on your neck. Wrong. It did nothing. Zip. The circles were fractionally paler, but they were still there. Leering out at me.

Second Attempt: Toothpaste. Toothpaste is whiter than concealer, right? And it's really hard to get off clothes so I figured it must have some pretty impressive covering capabilities. Wrong again. It's too different to skin colour so it really stands out, even if you blend it with a bit of foundation and blusher. Plus it has lots of sparkly flecks in it. And your neck ends up smelling suspiciously minty.

Third Attempt: Back to the trusty scarf. My light pink wool one was too thick to wear inside without questions being asked, but right at the bottom of my drawer was the thin, gauzy green one that Mum bought me for my birthday last year as it 'made my eyes pop'. Pop out their sockets in disgust. It is revolting. No one with any taste would be seen dead in it. But today, it would have to do. I double-wrapped it round my neck, securing it in place with a jaunty bow, and teamed it with a white shirt, collar up, and jeans.

When the clock finally struck eight and Mum barged her way in bearing a cup of passive aggressive tea, she was shocked to find me sitting up, fully dressed and halfway through *The Great Gatsby*. You can really get a lot done if you wake early. I think I might get up at this time every day.

'Oh... Morning, love.'

'Morning, Mum.'

'Ooh, you look nice. I told you that you'd change your mind about that scarf.'

The 6am start gave me time to gear up mentally for breakfast too. I had been on a date with a boy. A boy had picked me up from my house *and* I'd come home late. I didn't know how Dad would be taking it all. How close to cardiac arrest he'd be. I walked into the kitchen. He was sat with a mug of Nescafé and seemed ... weirdly fine. I took out a cereal bowl. Still fine. Skin tone normal. Poured in some Crunchy Nut Corn Flakes (a weekends-only treat on account of the 'high sugar content').

Dad finally reacted. But it wasn't an explosion of rage. More a sort of chuckle.

'Better not eat those around that Ennis.'

'What?!'

'Your mum told me about his allergic reaction. It'll be nuts. Peanuts, probably. Bound to be.'

'Dad, peanut allergies aren't funny. People die. Anna's brother has to carry an EpiPen with him.'

'I know, love, it's terrible.'

But the smile still hadn't completely gone. Ennis' hospitalisation had somehow turned him in Dad's mind from potential sex pest to the most harmless boy in the whole of Surrey. If he could be taken out by a peanut, then Andrew Smythe's daughter's honour was safe. The logic of a mad man. I worry sometimes that although I do pretty well at school, I can't actually be clever. There is no genetic basis whatsoever for me to be smart.

By lunchtime I was already knackered, the smugness had evaporated and the reality was starting to kick in: I could spend all weekend in a disgusting scarf, but what about Monday? I couldn't wear a scarf to school. Some evil teacher would whip it off before I was halfway through the front gates. I had to have a new plan. Something that would pass St Mary's draconian dress code. Could I claim it as an essential religious accessory? That I'd converted to a little-known C of E sect, which believes that to show one's neck in public is the most obscene blasphemy of all? Unlikely they'd buy it. I wracked my brain. Tina Reed had worn a neck brace last term. Where could I get a neck brace...?

Mum was busy in the garden. Attacking a plant with an over-sized pair of scissors. She claims 'gardening is a very mindful activity'. Plus, she'd sacked our gardener last month for being massively lazy. To be fair, she did have a point. At the far end of the garden a huge bramble bush had sprung up and was spreading forwards, triffid-style, towards the house. You didn't need a degree in Botany to know that it shouldn't be there. Maybe the whole place would end up shrouded in brambles and I'd get to sleep for a hundred years, by which time the bruises would have faded and the prince wouldn't think I looked really tacky.

'Mum,' I said, sidling up to her, my voice channelling newborn lamb, 'my neck hurts.'

'Oh.' She didn't even slow her pace. *Snip snip snip.*

'I think I've twisted it.'

'That sounds very unlikely.' *Snip snip snip.*

'I think I need a neck brace.'

'No you don't.' *Snip snip snip.*

So, the neck brace option was out.

The only other thing I could think of was a huge plaster. Or rather two huge plasters covering up the offending areas. But I couldn't just open up our first aid tin and stick plasters on my neck without a word of explanation. My mum would instantly yank them off again. I needed a reason. A cover story. I had to suffer a believable injury. Now, an actual cut was too extreme. What reason would there be for a knife or pair of open scissors to come anywhere near my neck? Couple that with the scenario in which I misjudged things and accidentally slit my throat and went down in history as suicide girl. No, it had to be a scratch. Something minor.

My reverie was interrupted by Dad yelling to my right. He was halfway up a step ladder, attempting, badly, to attach a trellis to the top of the fence.

'India, if you're not doing anything, why don't you get the secateurs and start work on the bramble bush?'

'Bramble bush … sure.'

Dad nearly fell off his ladder in surprise. I'd never shown the slightest interest in gardening before. Never offered to help pull a single dandelion from the lawn, let alone take out a bramble bush.

He didn't know what a gift he'd given me. A perfect, perfect gift.

Launching yourself into a bramble patch is a hard thing for your brain to make your body do.

*Jump legs*, it instructs, and the most they can manage is a lame curtsey style motion. Meghan Markle popping in for tea with the Queen. It was after five minutes of bobbing up and down that I had a revelation. I didn't actually need to fall into the brambles. I just had to claim that I had.

Swivelling my head, I scanned right and left across the garden. Mum was still focused – present, in the moment – snipping away, and Dad was balanced precariously at the top of the step ladder, with a hammer in one hand and a nail sticking out of his mouth. This was my chance.

'Aggghhhhh!' I yelled theatrically, dropping the secateurs and sprinting back towards the house, clutching my neck.

'What's going on?' from Mum, still snipping.

'Are you OK?' from Dad, still up the ladder.

Neither of them exactly sprinted to my aid. For all they knew I could have severed my jugular. It was a bit like that time when I was seven and fell into a stream and instead of diving in to save me, Mum just stood on the bank and flinched. I fought back the anger. Now was not a time for outrage. I had to remember I *wanted* them to stay put. I didn't want them to come racing to check out the non-existent damage.

'It's nothing serious.' I flung back. 'Just a couple of bramble scratches. I'm going to put a plaster on it.'

'Make sure you put some Savlon on first.'

'Will do.'

Safely inside the bathroom, I locked the door and pulled down the first aid box. There was a choice of two types of plaster. 'Thick and waterproof' sounded about right. I chose the two largest and then positioned myself in front of the mirror above the sink.

Peel and stick, peel and stick.

The scarf could come off.

I met up with Meena in the Fountain Centre in Rainston. She said she wanted to hang out and get a new neutral coloured lip gloss, but I knew that wasn't the real reason.

No, it was going to be an afternoon of being grilled about my date with Ennis. I'd refused to tell her all the details by text. I didn't want anything committed to writing. Not unless it was on a piece of rice paper that I could then crumple into a ball and swallow.

We went to Burger Burger Burger first. 'So good they named it thrice.' Meena's really into it. Everyone in my year is. It's *the* place to go. I hadn't been before, but, looking round, I really didn't get what all the fuss was about. There were reasonably cool retro booths, but the burgers themselves looked pretty much like McDonald's ones, so why spend about ten pounds rather than three? Maybe that's how they picked the name. *If we write 'burger' three times, people might not mind paying three times as much.* It made no sense. I ordered a cheeseburger with everything except mushrooms, waited for it to arrive and then claimed a booth.

Meena audibly snort-laughed as I removed my coat and scarf.

'What are those plasters?!'

'I scratched myself on some brambles.'

'Why don't you have scratches on your face or hands then?

Hmmm. Seems the rest of the population are not as easily fooled as my parents. It seems that my parents really aren't very bright. Which again probably means that I'm not actually very bright... I took a bite of my burger. I take it back. Burger Burger Burger burgers are delicious.

'Earth to India.'

'Sorry.'

Meena did a tiny frown and then her eyes suddenly expanded to fill most of her face.

'He gave you love bites, didn't he! O.M.G. Ennis gave you love bites!!!!'

It took the best part of an hour and an extra portion of chips for the whole ugly truth to come spilling out. And to reach love bites we had to journey via Elephant Man, hospital and Mum texting Ennis.

Meena looked like she'd never enjoyed herself so much.

'You're like – hahahahaha – some – hahahahaha – femme fatale poisoner – hahahahaha!!!!!!!!!!'

'It probably wasn't even my fault. How can you be allergic to perfume *and* wear Lynx?!?'

'What was the name of the perfume again?'

'*Lucky.*'

'*Lucky*? Hahahhahahahaha!!!!!!!!!!'

'Stop it.'

'OK, OK. Wait a minute…' Meena pulled out her phone and started tapping away. '*Lucky*… Russian perfume … withdrawn from the market after a month … found to include several toxic irritants. Hahahahhahahahaha!!!!!!!!!'

She showed me the page. My worst fears confirmed.

'Don't worry. He won't find out. Has he been in touch since?'

I shook my head.

'Nothing.'

'What about your Mum? Has she heard from him? Hahahahahahaha!!!!!!!! Sorry, I couldn't resist that.'

I stared daggers at her and watched her face fight itself as she tried to get it under control and look contrite.

'Oh well.' Meena had switched to 'comforting' mode, trying to sound reassuring and failing, totally. 'I'm sure it won't be too awkward tomorrow.'

'Tomorrow?'

'*Tomorrow* – the Consent workshops?'

Bollocks.

Bollocks. Bollocks. Bollocks.

In all the stress I'd totally forgotten. Earlier in the year some moron teacher at St Mary's had met up with some moron teacher at St Joseph's and decided: *Wouldn't it be a great idea in the current climate if the Year 10 teens from both schools workshopped their way through some tricky consent issues? Boys and girls. Feeling their way together. Each understanding the other's perspective. In a challenging and educational environment.* Which meant that I was going to have to spend the whole morning in the same room as the guy who'd chewed up my neck, who I'd nearly suffocated and who my mum had sent rude texts to.

'Shall we get another Coke Zero?' Meena suggested.

Yes, I replied. 'I think that's for the best.'

At 8:57pm I got a text from Ennis: 'Sorry fri night ended so badly. Let's not tell anyone, right? See you tmrw. What are you doing next fri?'

He didn't hate me.

He was embarrassed. He probably thought not being able to breathe unaided somehow impacted on his masculinity.

And he wanted to see me again.

I tried to digest these thoughts, but they stayed whole, a lump, knotting in my stomach like Mum's three bean casserole.

The one good thing. The one really good thing that I could grab hold of and wrap my arms round like a comfort blanket was that Lisa and April wouldn't know. Ennis wouldn't tell them anything.

Beeep Beeep Beeep Beeep!!!!!!

Through sleep-blurred eyes, the horrific, glowing digits 6:30 slowly came into focus. What? They should say 7:00. Why the hell don't they say 7:00!?!!!! Then my brain began to turn on too. My alarm was set for thirty minutes *earlier* than normal so that I could go to school looking considerably *better* than normal.

My typical weekday morning routine involves hitting the snooze button three times followed by chucking my school uniform on, eating a bowl of (less than 5% sugar) Cheerios, the only ones Mum will now buy for weekdays, a quick face wash, teeth brush, some attempt at taming my crazy hair and then, if there's time, mixing a bit of Max Factor Ivory colour-match foundation into my moisturiser for a better-than-nature-intended complexion.

Today, however, was not a typical day. We were going to be at St Joseph's and I was Ennis's... girl. I was going to be stared at, examined, judged. Normal me wouldn't cut it.

I was down for breakfast before Mum and Dad so no one was there to yell at me as I sprinkled two teaspoons of sugar on my Cheerios, restoring them to their former glory. Feeling a hundred times better, I bounded back up the stairs and began work on my face. This was definitely a foundation undiluted by moisturiser day. Plus a bit of lip gloss. Plus subtle mascara. I considered leaving my hair down but then looked out the window and inwardly chuckled at my near catastrophic error. There was a fine drizzle and fine drizzle + my hair = bouffant nightmare. I grabbed a hairband instead and after four attempts ended up with a not too terrible ponytail – one that straddled that fine line of acceptability between overly falling out and Betty Cooper from *Riverdale*. Final check in the mirror – left side, right side, close-up on forehead and side of the nose and chin: no spots, thank you, God. The plasters on my neck looked pretty stupid, but there was nothing that I could do about that. At least they were firmly stuck down. Not a love bite in sight.

I was ready. Ready to take on the day.

Even though the workshops were going to be at St Joseph's, morning register was still at St Mary's. Meena was already in our classroom when I arrived, looking significantly better than normal. She must have gone all out and braved a 6am alarm, or, potentially even a 5:30.

To be fair, everyone in the class was looking pretty

good – it was almost freaky, like we'd somehow morphed into a different reality. A new and improved 10J. Even Mrs Johnson, who normally sticks to clothes in different shades of rodent, had put on a pink top and quite a bright shade of lipstick. An error, it turns out, as it brought attention to her overly small top lip. My stomach started to twist and flip from the weirdness of it all when in bumbled Anna. Thank God for Anna. Glasses on as always (even though she has slight astigmatism and would actually see better in contact lenses), not a trace of make-up, hair savagely parted and tucked behind her ears, and – the cherry on top – a large, white splodge of what must have been cold sore cream balancing on the top right corner of her mouth. Space trip over. All was right in the world.

'Quiet now, 10J.' Mrs Johnson's voice cut across the room. She was one of those teachers people actually listened to. She'd never be locked out of a temporary classroom.

'This morning is not some *jolly*. It is a serious, important exercise. You may be at St Joseph's but you will still be representing St Mary's. How you conduct yourselves will reflect back on this school. And the rules of this school still apply.'

Lisa was rolling her eyes when Mrs Johnson pounced.

'Lisa Hartley, what is this school's policy on make-up?'

'Um.'

'Speak up, I can't hear you.'

'No make-up should be worn, Mrs Johnson,' Lisa chanted back.

'Exactly. A fact that ninety-nine percent of you seem to have forgotten. You will each be given a wet wipe, which you will then use to remove all traces of make-up from your face. Anyone failing to do this will receive an immediate detention.'

No, no, no, NO!!!!!!!!!!!!

A wet wipe was going to destroy everything. It was going to take me from an eight to a six-point-five instantly. Goodbye cheekbones. Goodbye larger-than-normal-looking eyes. Hello pale, sallow skin. I wasn't alone in my distress. Cries of despair rent the air like we were a flock of seagulls who'd just spied a kid with a Cornish pasty. Could Mrs Johnson really be this cruel?

Apparently so. She was already pulling wet wipes from a packet and handing them out. They hung limply from girls' hands, like flags of surrender.

Slowly the glamour was being rubbed from the room. Traces of pimples, blotchy skin, dark eye bags all reappeared. A reversed *before* and *after* advert. *Wet wipes: you didn't know you could look THIS bad!* Anna stared at her wet wipe, bemused, before eventually using it to clean her hands. Mrs Johnson got to keep her lipstick though. The rules conveniently didn't apply to her.

A far less confident 10J was shepherded out of the room, through the school gates, down the one hundred metres of pavement and in through St Joseph's gates. It was the first time I'd actually set foot in St Joseph's and it felt weird. Smelt weird. The air in the corridors was an overpowering blend of testosterone, stale socks and Lynx. *Lucky* must be properly toxic if Ennis could inhale this every day and be absolutely fine.

Anna seemed perfectly at home as she came every Thursday after school for orchestra practice. This was her home-from-home turf. Meena also looked relatively comfortable. Her older brother, Guv, went here. It was just me who was staring round, bug-eyed, exploring an alien planet.

The Consent Workshops were taking place in the hall. It was the only room big enough to fit in all of our year group as well as their Year 10s. My heart was hammering against my ribcage as Mrs Johnson flung open the double doors and started ushering us inside. The boys were there already. Hanging around in groups. Staring at us as we filed in. It felt like one of those markets for evacuees during the war. Does anyone want to take this one home? Anyone?

I spotted Ennis in the corner with Anthony and a couple of other guys I didn't know. He smiled and winked, seemingly pleased to see me. But he didn't come over. Was I supposed to go over to him? Or didn't he want to be seen with me? I sort of froze on the spot like an idiot, saved only by one of the St Joseph's teachers ringing a bell and then other teachers marching around, dividing us into groups of twenty. I was in 'Purple' group with Meena (good) and April (bad). Anna told me later that she'd heard that they'd originally named the groups after films but then it'd turned out that over half the films contained actors who'd #MeToo-ed people so they'd reverted to colours last minute.

Most of the guys looked OK. A bit spotty but not lechy or total neeks at all.

'It's so unfair that Ennis and Anthony are in a different group,' April pouted.

'Er … yes,' I replied, secretly massively relieved that I wasn't going to role play 'tricky consent issues' around Ennis.

*May I give you some really big, tacky love bites?*

*No, actually, you may not.*

Lost in thought, I didn't really register when a teacher came over, propelling another guy into our group. Next minute, I felt a tap on my shoulder and span round to come face to face with curly hair, blue eyes and a weirdly high forehead: Rich Evans.

'Hi India. Oh, sorry, did I startle you?'

'No, hi, yes, a bit, but it's OK.'

'I was sort of hoping you'd be in my group.'

'…me too,' I'd formed the words from politeness, but as they came out my mouth, I realised I actually meant them. And not in the hashtag way. I was genuinely pleased that Rich Evans was with me.

'Who's this?' April hissed, suddenly at my elbow. She covers ground like a ninja serpent. 'I don't believe we've met.'

'Oh. Um. Hi, April, I'm Rich. Rich Evans. I actually met you at Anthony's

party.'

'Oh yes, that makes sense.' And a weird, cruel little smile formed on April's lips.

April, quickly losing interest in us lesser beings, ninja slithered her way back to the other side of the group and began working her charms on the best-looking guy available. He looked like he was going to swallow his Adam's apple in excitement.

I could feel my muscles physically relax with every step away that she took.

'Was your Dad OK after the party?' Rich whispered.

'He went ape for a while but things have calmed down now, thanks.'

'Cool. I was worried about you.' Pause. 'You look nice, by the way.'

'Thanks. I could have looked loads better but our evil teacher made us remove our make-up.'

'Well, as someone who's seen you in make-up and without, I can honestly say that you look better now.' There was a twinkle in his blue eyes. He was teasing me. I do believe I was flirting with Rich Evans.

'This morning's going to be ridiculous,' I whispered back.

'I know. What guy really needs to be told not to grope girls?' His eyes were now super earnest as they stared into mine. My breath semi-caught. We were definitely having a moment. When he looked down at me, the perspective even made his forehead look normal sized. A beat, and then he continued. 'I mean I'd never touch you.'

'Oh. Right. Nice to know.'

Moment over.

'Unless you wanted me to and then I'd be all over you.'

'Oh.'

'God, that came out all wrong.'

We sat for an awkward few seconds of silence until Mr Grange from St Joseph's introduced himself and called for quiet. We were all supposed to face the front for a whole-group discussion before we then broke off for smaller role play exercises within our groups.

Mr Grange then proceeded to drone on about consent and 'no meaning no' and 'silence not being the same as consent' for twenty minutes. It wasn't *what* he said – that was obviously all really important stuff – it was just the *way* he said it: a mash-up of totally boring and super embarrassing. When he said 'puberty', 'hormones' and 'sexual stirrings' in rapid succession, a collective cringe spread round the hall like a Mexican wave.

'Before we start a role play, does anyone have any questions?'

April's hand shot up. She had her snake eyes on. Beware teacher, beware.

'Yes?' Mr Grange nodded at her, inviting her to speak. He was smiling, glad of the participation. It was beyond obvious that he'd never met April before. And dangerous reptile identification was clearly not his forte.

'Time for some fun,' April whispered to the boy in her thrall. 'Mr Grange, you suggested that silence might not be sufficient to indicate consent.'

'Er … yes.'

'What about for someone mute? Are you suggesting that a mute person should never be allowed to have sex?! That's so offensive!'

'No. No. That's not what I was suggesting at all. In this … particular case … consent might be shown in a different way.'

'Like through sign language?' April suggested, helpfully.

'Yes. Yes, sign language. Exactly.'

'What sign language would you use to demonstrate consent?'

'Er…' Mr Grange was properly floundering now. All eyes were fixed on him. What would he come up with? 'Er … maybe a clear nod of the head.'

The whole hall broke into hysterics with everyone doing exaggerated head nods at each other.

Mrs Johnson stormed onto the stage to replace Mr Grange.

'Quiet, NOW! Year 10, these are serious issues we're dealing with. Please give them the respect that they deserve. Mr Grange has designed a simple exercise for us, which we'll demonstrate on stage first. We need a girl and a boy.' April's hand shot up and Mrs Johnson shot her a withering laser glare. A lesser girl would have spontaneously combusted, leaving a small pile of ash on the floor.

'I'm not going to ask for volunteers, I'll just pick. We'll use you,' Mrs Johnson pointed at Gillian, 'and you,' her finger singled out Anthony. 'Come up onto the stage, please.'

Interesting choices. Anthony, one of the most rated guys at St Joseph's and … Gillian. Tall, broad, sport-obsessed and with a monobrow to rival Frida Kahlo's. Gillian has never shown even the slightest bit of interest in boys. Nor girls for that matter. She might be tempted to dry hump a netball, but that'd be about it.

'Mr Grange, would you like to explain how this works?' Mrs Johnson was determined to keep the morning on track.

A redder, sweatier Mr Grange returned to the stage.

'R-r-right,' he spluttered. 'So the boy is going to approach the girl, thinking that she is interested and the girl is going to calmly and clearly let the boy know that she isn't.'

'The girls are always interested,' Anthony boasted and about four guys from his group crowed. Literally puffed out their chests, made a crowing noise and high-fived each other. Horrific. Totally horrific. Some guys definitely need to attend a Consent Workshop.

'That's not quite the attitude we're looking for here, is it?' said Mr Grange, trying desperately to assert himself. 'Now, let's move on with the exercise. Anthony, please approach Gillian.'

Anthony swaggered a few steps towards Gillian, his hips rivalling April's for bendiness.

'All right?' he said.

That's when Gillian swung into action.

Sticking out her hand in a policeman-stopping-traffic

gesture, she opened her mouth and bellowed. 'Come any closer and I'll kick you in the dick. I will kick you in the dick.'

Anthony was frozen to the spot in terror. Gillian raised her knee and the kick was clearly coming, when Mr Grange flew in to intervene.

'Right. Well. That was clear and … forceful. Maybe a little *too* forceful. But yes, you see the general point. OK, change of plan. We're not going to role play that particular issue again; we're going to break for a drink and a biscuit and then resume in ten minutes.'

Sweat was now literally dripping off Mr Grange's forehead and he disappeared off stage in search of a paper towel and face deodorant.

Everyone was nearly wetting themselves with laughter and as we headed over to the refreshments table Meena whispered in my ear, 'Best. Morning. Ever.'

The queue at the table was massive, but Rich appeared by my side clutching four glasses of orange squash, with a fistful of Bourbons balanced on a napkin on top.

'For you and your friends,' he said, shyly. St Joseph's was clearly less tight than St Mary's. Apart from in the library, we always have water and rich tea biscuits. Meena smiled her thanks and Anna bumbled over to join us. Rich fitted right in. It was like he was one of the gang. Like you couldn't even tell that he was a boy, not that he was in any way particularly feminine or anything – just that everyone acted normal. Meena didn't feel the need to flick her hair every five seconds and Anna, well Anna was Anna.

Ennis didn't come over. I had one ear and one eye open for him. Ready for his advance. But it didn't happen. He was at the other end of the hall, too cool for squash and biscuits, flanked by Anthony and Lisa and April.

I felt pissed off and relieved in equal measure. Finally, just as I was heading back to the Purple group section, he sidled up, slipped his hand round my waist, squeezed, and whispered, 'Hey, India,' into my ear and was off again.

What the hell I was supposed to make of that, I don't know.

'Oh my God, did you see what Ennis just did?' Rich exploded at my side. 'He just … touched you … he just … grabbed you! Do you want me to have a word with him?' He was opening and closing his right fist and a vein was pulsing in his forehead. My knight in shining armour. This is the moment I should have told him. It would have been simple enough. *Rich, that waist squeezer, is my sort of boyfriend.* But for some reason I didn't want to. Didn't want Rich to know. So instead I mumbled a lame, 'No, don't worry, ha ha, I don't think that happened. I didn't notice anything.' Which seemed to leave Rich stunned and probably trying to work out exactly how fat my waist must be if it was unable to detect a fly-by squeeze.

After the break we had to workshop 'signs of interest and disinterest' using these terrible worksheets. They covered 'verbal and non-verbal clues' and we were supposed to talk through them slowly and seriously. Obviously that didn't happen. April's latest boy toy, the Adam Apple Swallower, looked like he might have a coronary as she stroked his arm and then his leg, all the time cooing into his ear, 'Does this seem like I'm interested?' At one point he backed away, crossed his legs and had a semi-choking coughing fit.

I was paired with Rich, and we'd got onto the 'non-verbal' section. He kept staring at my knee like he wasn't sure whether to try and touch it or not.

Looking round the hall, it was like everyone had gone into slow motion. All these guys and girls were starting to touch each other. Hands on arms. Hands on legs. Three pairs had started snogging.

'STOP! STOP THIS NOW!' Mrs Johnson flung herself onto the stage, an action hero bodyguard, jumping in the way of a bullet. Bubbles of spittle were collecting at the corners of her mouth. It was like she'd caught rabies.

'This moral degeneracy will end now. St Mary's girls, you will all proceed to the end of the hall THIS INSTANT and we will return to school. You are a disgrace. DISGRACE!!!!!!!'

As I stood up to leave, Rich tugged me down.

'India?'

'What? I've got to go.'

'Do you want to come out with me on Friday?' he began. 'Not just me,' he added quickly as if worried he'd been too full on. 'Me and some friends. Would you like to?'

Friday. I was supposed to be seeing Ennis on Friday.

I saw Rich's face fall as I hesitated.

'Don't worry. It's fine,' he said, trying to sound all upbeat.

'No … no, it's just Friday is tricky. Friday's not good for me.'

'How about the Recital? Come to the Christmas Recital? I'm singing. Mr Hopper's chosen me for the last number – the audience participation bit. Fancy coming onto the stage and singing with me?'

My brain returned to that assembly. Singing in front of the school. All things bright and beautiful.

'Never. No way. No.'

'OK. OK,' Rich laughed. 'I get the message. No singing. But come anyway. Please?'

'India! India Smythe!' Mrs Johnson's voice hammered down on me before I had a chance to answer. 'The end of the hall, now.'

'I've got to go,' I whispered to Rich.

And this time I went.

On the walk back to St Mary's I must have had a stupid grin on my face as next thing I knew, Meena was grabbing hold of my arm and whispering in my ear.

'Why do you have a stupid grin on your face? You don't fancy Rich Evans, do you?'

'No, no, of course not.'

But I could tell from Meena's now permanently raised left eyebrow, like a Botox job gone horribly wrong, that she didn't believe me.

'Why were you flirting with him all morning then?'

'Was not!'

'Well, don't do anything stupid, OK?'

We reached the front gates and I paused.

'But you like him, don't you, Meena? I thought you liked Rich.'

'I do. I *like* him. But you're supposed to be with Ennis, aren't you? Ennis is A-list. Rich is C-list at best.

You don't cheat on As with Cs. And think about Lisa and April. They'd crucify you.'

Meena was right. In Year 7, Sarah Green had done something minor to slight April. Accidentally trod on her new trainers or something. April hadn't reacted immediately like a normal person would. Instead, the next day she'd invited Sarah to sit next to her at lunch. Sarah had accepted, embarrassingly gratefully, thinking this was a gesture of forgiveness. A 1pm olive branch. It wasn't. April slipped an open ketchup sachet on the seat just before Sarah sat down and then told everyone that Sarah had her period and had bled all over her skirt.

That was for treading on a trainer.

Packed lunch disaster.

Mum, having rewatched *Blue Planet* one too many times, has decided that as a household we're going PLAHstic free. No more PLAHstic bags. No more cling film. We are going to get milk delivered in glass bottles. Fruit and vegetables in paper bags from the greengrocer. Our sandwiches will be wrapped in greaseproof paper secured by reuseable rubber bands. All very good in theory. I'm not totally evil. I don't sit around in high-backed chairs, stroking white cats and practising my *mwah haw haw* while planning environmental destruction. I'm as much in favour of non-toxic oceans and leaping dolphins as the next person. However, when my normally securely cling film wrapped tuna mayo and cucumber sandwich exploded out of its greaseproof paper and rubber band home, shedding blobs of stinky, gloopy brown fish all over my books and deep into the seams of my school bag's lining, David Attenborough may have fallen ever so slightly in my estimation.

Mum announced our plastic-free future last night at dinner. And she's not just stopping with our household. Mum's getting political. Which in itself is a miracle. She and Dad don't do politics. They've pretty much stopped watching the news altogether since the Brexit fiasco. They decided it'd be better for their relationship. The months before their self-imposed news embargo these terrible sighs and groans would escape from the living room punctuated with the odd shouted phrase:

'Hatchet faced harpy!'

'Bloody commie … wants to turn us into Venez-effing-uela.'

So the big news is that Mum's decided to spend her Thursday mornings campaigning against plastic waste in the High Street. A group of local mums and dads are doing it. It's like the new yoga. Bit of group chanting followed by a flat white. I was pretty proud of Mum when she first mentioned it. Mum actually doing something for a worthy cause. That was until she stood up from the table to 'demonstrate the chant'.

'Say NO and GO to PLAHstic,

The ocean's limits aren't ELAHstic.

So don't wrap-de-wrap-de-wrap it,

In non-biodegradable PLAHstic.'

This, accompanied by pumping arms, a shaking finger and weird leg thrusts.

'You'll get a better idea how it all comes together when I'm in my active wear,' she added, hammering a final nail into the coffin.

Dad and I both just sat there, staring, in pure, frozen, open-mouthed horror. The odd PLAHstic bag or ELAHstic band at home or in front of friends was bad enough, but *this,* chanted in front of the world, with actions. This was too much.

'Um … I thought you had Pilates on Thursday?' Dad ventured gingerly. 'You *love* Pilates.'

'No. Linda, Jo and I decided this was more important. And it's going to be good exercise too. Linda was thinking we could even turn the actions into more of a dance routine. She's working with this move she saw on *Strictly*.'

I couldn't take it any more. A single, simple, 'NO!' exploded from my mouth and hovered over the kitchen table, a weaponised drone. Mum didn't move or say anything for five seconds, but then burst into tears and stormed off.

'Look what you've done, you've upset your mother,' Dad shouted at me, projecting his voice to ensure the words followed Mum into whichever room she'd disappeared off to. Then his eyes flickered to the door and he semi-whispered at a quarter of his previous volume, 'You don't think she'll go ahead with it, do you?'

It was about an hour after this that Mum made and wrapped my tuna and cucumber sandwich. I have a feeling she sabotaged it on purpose.

April and Lisa asked me to the Fence today. They marched up to my table, ten minutes into lunch and told me to hurry up, we had plans to finalise for Friday. My first thought was: *wait a minute, I'm only halfway through my cheese sandwich* (made by yours truly and brought buried in a Tupperware coffin). I have no idea how they get through lunch so quickly. Come to think of it, I don't think I've ever seen them eat anything. Maybe they've bypassed normal human evolution and learnt to photosynthesise. I hope so. It would be awesome if they ended up turning green.

My second thought, which quickly steamrolled over the first, crushing it to nothing, was: *Friday night is going to be a group thing. I'm not ready for a group thing.* I was nervous enough about another date with Ennis, let alone seeing him with April and Lisa there. Watching, judging. I hadn't even spoken to him since the Consent Workshops, and even then, a quick waist squeeze probably doesn't rate high up the list of communication methods. OK, he'd sent me two texts as well: Monday eve: *All right babe?* Wednesday eve: *Looking fwd to fri night. Kiss emoji.* But that was it. We weren't going to be winning any prizes at the *Great Conversations of the Month Awards.*

Stuffing the rest of my cheese sandwich into my mouth and munching an apple as we walked, April and Lisa escorted me to the Fence. It was quite hard keeping time with them, as I don't naturally swish from side to side when I walk. The swishing bit took up about half a second per step, so I was either too fast or too slow. I scanned left and right as we approached. The thought I couldn't shake was *please don't let Rich Evans see me.*

'Hey babe.' Anthony greeted April and they seamlessly managed their usual through the Fence snog.

I drew level with Ennis. He winked and then stared at me expectantly, slowly beginning to angle his head and lean in towards the wire. The signal couldn't be clearer. We were going to do an Anthony and April too. The pinnacle of social success. Meena would be so proud.

OK. OK. I could do this. I just had to position my lips in the middle of a diamond of wire. That was it. How hard could it be? As a kid I was a master of Operation – I basically never let the hoop touch the wire and never got zapped. April, on the other hand, always drops the ball in netball and got 34% in our last Physics test, so she was unlikely to be a master of spatial awareness and lip-position engineering.

I titled my head to a forty-five degree angle and began to lean in.

Attempt number one, and my nose bumped into the wire cross joint and rebounded with a painful, swallowed, 'Ow!'

Attempt number two, and I nearly took out my right eye.

Attempt number three, and I managed to get the angle right. Head tilted more like sixty degrees clockwise, knees slightly bent, lips through the diamond. Ennis's lips were in position on the other side, but weren't exactly poking through. To actually reach them,

I had to push my face into the wire. We broke apart after ten seconds. How Anthony and April find that enjoyable I have no idea.

As I recaught my breath, I noticed that Ennis was staring at me. At my face. After a couple of seconds he burst into laughter. What? I swivelled round to Lisa and April and they tinkled away too, but in a minor key that told me if there hadn't been guys there, they would have been having a go at me about something. Eventually, Ennis stopped chortling enough to explain. Apparently, I'd pressed my face too far into the wire and now had a diamond shaped imprint surrounding my mouth. Excellent. Truly excellent.

'You're so funny, India,' Ennis smiled.

Hilarious. Just hilarious.

'So where are we going, Friday?' Lisa chimed in, keen to draw the attention in her direction. 'The Green?'

No please, not the Green again!

'No, s'too cold,' Ennis replied. His eyes had suddenly taken on a haunted look. I don't think he ever wanted to return to the Green again. He probably had a funny turn every time he heard an ambulance siren too. 'How about yours, Anthony?'

'Nope, my 'rentals are both home. How about we go loser spotting?'

'Love it,' tinkled April.

'OK,' Anthony confirmed. 'Loser spotting it is.'

Anthony and April had a final quick goodbye snog while me and Ennis kind of just nodded at each other formally.

'Laterz,' Ennis smiled and winked, turning away.

This time I remembered not to say 'laterz' back.

My face doesn't suit no sleep. It looked like someone had inflated the section round my eyes, beach lilo style.

It had rained solidly last night – that sort of driving rain that hits the window panes and sounds like some evil mass murderer is tapping away, trying to get in.

People who claim to sleep amazingly to the sound of rain are either liars or totally lack imagination.

It was still raining at breakfast.

Mum had her active wear on. Dad was eating his Cheerios (which incidentally he'd smothered in honey, taking their sugar content up to about 35%) and kept shooting looks at Mum and opening and then closing his mouth, clearly deciding whether or not to risk asking something. He does this whenever he thinks she might freak out at him. Like when he wants to go away for the weekend with Kev 'from the band' who she thinks is a bad influence and is trying to lure him away from the world of dentistry back to late nights, no money and bad hairstyles.

'Samantha?'

'What, love?'

'You look nice.'

'What do you want?' Mum lacks a lot of self-awareness, but she's not a complete fool.

'Are you still planning on protesting this morning? You know, with the rain and everything?'

Mum chewed her bite of bagel for literally fifteen seconds before replying. There is no way a piece of bagel takes that long to eat. She was definitely deliberately torturing him.

'I think I might go to Pilates instead,' she replied eventually.

Dad semi-collapsed onto his stool in relief.

'Whatever you feel like, love.'

Mum. Protector of the world's oceans. Except when it's raining. Maybe she thought the extra water would somehow dilute the problem.

Double Art again today. I was double-crossing my fingers on the walk down the corridor, hoping that Mr Major had made a speedy recovery and Ms Roberts would be gone. Taken her too short fringe and orange lipstick back to Whitechapel.

No such luck. She was sitting on the desk as we filed

in. Not behind it. On it. As if that somehow made her this super-cool rule breaker rather than a totally predictable loser who was flashing too much fishnet covered thigh.

'Today, class,' she began, with a melodramatic inhalation, 'we're going to explore. Reinvent. *Discover.*'

Which meant absolutely nothing.

'We're going to continue the theme from your workshops on Monday of self-respect, of personal space, of consent, and I want you to discover what 'strong female role model' means to you.

Meena did an exaggerated biceps flex and a snort laugh just exploded out of my nose. The next moment, I had Ms Robert's orange lips moving around close up like a siren. 'Do you have something you'd like to say, India?'

'No, Miss.'

'Ms.'

'No, Ms.'

'Good. Keep your focus on the task at hand. I want you producing something more exciting today. Nothing tame and derivative.'

Tame and derivative. I had to fight back another snort. I'll give you tame and derivative Mssssssssss most derivative 'artist' ever. I bet she even had an oversized yellow wool coat somewhere, or – if not – was saving up for one when she next sold a painting.

I'd got to Art late so I wasn't ensconced in a protective huddle of friends. I had Meena to my right, but to the left was Gillian. I felt like that penguin at the edge of the iceberg that's not going to make it through the winter.

What to produce? I literally had no ideas. It wasn't that I disliked the theme. I am totally behind the idea of strong females, obviously. It was just that the pressure of having to prove myself to Ms Roberts was crushing any creative spirit. Meena had decided to go all colourful again – if it ain't broke… She'd drawn a red stick woman in the middle of an A3 piece of paper and was now basically just splashing blobs of colour round it.

'What's that to do with strong female role model?' I giggled.

'Not sure yet,' she replied. 'But it's really fun.'

To my left, Gillian was attacking a piece of paper with a piece of charcoal.

'What's you plan?' I whispered to her. This is what I was reduced to. Asking Miss Sports-loving-zero-interest-in-Art for advice.

'Self-portrait,' Gillian replied gruffly. I nodded my respect. Good call. Gillian had certainly proved herself to be a strong female. And if anyone disagreed, she could always kick them in the dick.

I picked up a pastel set and sat facing my paper.

Strong female role model… Well it probably had to be a person. Someone who fought for women's rights. That's it. Flashbulb moment, I'd draw a suffragette. Chaining herself to some railings so that future women would get to have a say in whether the country was run by a Hell Harpy or Bloodie Commie.

'You have twenty more minutes,' Ms Roberts decreed, re-crossing her legs on the desk. Great, another uncalled for flash. It was like being at a compulsory burlesque performance.

I ignored Meena's attempts to start a conversation, blocked out Anna's waves from across the room and instead put all my focus into the task at hand. Using a mix of brown, white and pink pastels I captured a face, fringed with ringlets, raised in supplication. I stole from the Pre-Raphaelites, from Botticelli. The neck was delicate and elongated a la Modigliani, the body encased in a limiting, structured dress of the time. Metal handcuffs circled the wrists, digging into them, leaving the skin cut and raw.

'And stop!'

Ms Roberts began her classroom prowl, looking for work to praise or pull apart. Anna's was 'interesting' – a green triangle perched on top of a blue square. I managed to avoid eye contact. Laughing now would not be a good move. Sammy's – which looked like a man in drag – was 'subversive'. April's – basically a fashion model sketch – 'poor'. Finally she was at my row.

She reached Gillian's first.

'I like it. I really like it. You've clearly taken inspiration from Frida Kahlo. The eyebrows: exaggerated, unfeminine, grotesque almost – you're saying: *Men, I do not conform to your archaic system of beauty*, is that right?'

Then Ms Roberts looked up. Looked Gillian in the eye. Or rather the brow. And gulped. I don't think she'd ever seen Gillian close-up before. Not properly. Not gauged the full intensity of the monobrow.

'No, Miss,' Gillian replied coldly, never breaking eye contact. 'It's just a self-portrait. Of me.'

'Right.'

Ms Roberts flushed scarlet, her skin massively clashing with her lipstick. She let the 'Miss' slide. The 'Miss' was the least of her worries right now.

Gillian, you beautiful, beautiful creature. I could kiss you right now.

Like any fundamentally weak person who's been made to feel small, Ms Roberts looked around for a replacement victim. She didn't have to look far.

'And what have you drawn, India? A girl in a pretty dress? Really? Is that what you think a strong female role model is? Ha! You and April are so alike.'

There was a splutter of disbelief from April's bench.

'It's a suffragette!' I cried, determined to defend myself this time. 'She's chaining herself to a railing!' But the bell drowned out my words and Ms Roberts stalked off, leaving me packing up, burning with rage. I'm almost surprised the fire alarm didn't go off.

School was weird today. Exhausting. I felt like a ping-pong ball must feel at the end of a game after being whacked forwards and backwards over a net for ages.

Anna had had orchestra last night and dragged me off to a corner of the playing field in first break to tell me that she'd spoken loads to Rich last night and that he was really into me and that I had to ignore Meena, dump Ennis and go for the good guy instead.

'Ennis is Ed Sheeran whereas Rich is Tchaikovsky, if you know what I mean?'

'No Anna, I don't. Ennis isn't a pale, ginger guy and, last time I looked, Rich wasn't a dead Russian. Plus, Ed Sheeran seems really nice and he's massively successful, so wouldn't that logically mean that choosing Ed Sheeran was actually a good move?'

Anna shook her head with an annoyingly smug

smile, like she'd made such an erudite point that it had flown totally over my head.

'Sorry – bad choice of analogy – I forgot you were a music muggle for a moment.'

Yeah, because the orchestra is full of wizards.

Then at lunch it was Meena's turn to bundle me off – this time to a corner of the loos – far less classy – and tell me, in between suspicious looks to check all the cubicles were empty, that she'd definitely heard Lisa whisper the word 'ice sculpture' and 'next Saturday' to April in the middle of double History.

'And?' I asked wearily.

'Don't you see,' she hissed, exasperated. 'The Christmas Party. It's next Saturday. It's going to be amazing. Are you doing anything then?'

'Nothing much,' I replied.

'Well, play it right and you're going. You're going as Ennis's girlfriend!!!!!!!!'

And I hate to admit it, but a little frisson of excitement tingled its way up and down my spine.

Friday night and I was on the bus to Rainston to meet Ennis and everyone at Burger Burger Burger. (Lisa's choice. I was a bit surprised. She doesn't seem like a burger sort of person). Then we were going to hang out in World of Bowl – *Europe's premier bowling experience*. With only five lanes and bowling shoes that smell thirty years old, they could definitely get done by Trading Standards for false advertising/blatant lies, but Trading Standards probably couldn't be bothered to come this far into Surrey. And if they did, they'd probably also investigate Amps – *Europe's most electrifying discotheque*. So, burger then bowling – the sort of evening I've had all the time with Meena and Anna without getting weird heart palpitation flutters and bits of acid rising up my throat.

The thing is, I wasn't meeting Meena and Anna. I was meeting Lisa, April, Anthony and Ennis (who may or may not be my boyfriend) for an evening of 'ironic fun'.

The biggest irony so far was that Mum and Dad seemed perfectly happy for me to go. When Dad first heard the group I was meeting included A BOY he went typically mad.

Dad:  It'd better not be that pervert from the party.
Me:  Dad, Rich Evans isn't a pervert. He's a really nice guy.
[A noise like Dad was snorting his entire face up his left nostril.]

Me:    And it's not Rich I'm meeting anyway. It's Ennis.

Dad:   Ennis? [Face like a thundercloud.]

Mum:   Andrew, you remember, I told you. He's the boy India had to take to hospital after he suffered that terrible allergic reaction to peanuts or something. Sweet boy. We text occasionally.

*WHAT!?!*

But this wasn't the time to get into it.

Dad:   Oh, right. Peanut Boy. [A smile spread over Dad's face.] 'OK. But don't get back later than eleven-thirty.'

Eleven-thirty!! A result. This was the latest I'd ever been officially allowed out. In a short skirt too.

Back to the bus. We were passing the youth centre on Hawthorn Drive. Two more stops to go. I checked the shoulders of my coat for dandruff. Meena had given me a list of last-minute checks to do before I arrived. Dandruff was number one.

Tick.

So far so good. No unsightly visible flakes, but there were nine long hairs I had to remove. Did my hair normally moult this fast? Surely not? I'd checked my coat before I left and it had been hair free. Nine hairs for a fifteen-minute bus ride. It must be the stress. If it kept up at this rate then I'd lose thirty-six hairs an hour, which would make one hundred and eight hairs over a three hour date! I'd go bald! Bald, with really hairy shoulders. And this wasn't just paranoia. You hear talk of people who lose all their hair after some horrific incident. Even their eyebrow hair. That better not be happening right now. Bella Herbert's mum draws her eyebrows on with a brown crayon and looks ridiculous. Almost as bad as Tina Farmer's mum who started getting Botox last year and now permanently looks slightly surprised. A school play – how slightly surprising. A parents' evening – how slightly surprising. A school fete – you get my drift.

I desperately tried to push baldness to the back of my mind and focused again on the list.

Item number two – teeth.

I produced a pocket mirror and flashed a grimace at it. Lucky save. Thank you, Meena! A tiny piece of green lettuce from an afternoon sandwich was caught between my left lateral incisor and my canine. I know the names of all the different teeth. Dad taught me one summer. He was going through a phase of wanting to pass on some knowledge to his offspring, some fatherly wisdom. And since I was disappointingly not a boy and had no interest in Lego, football, cricket or the guitar, he resorted to dentistry instead.

Piece of green gone, it was time for item number three – breath. There was no sure way of testing whether my breath was OK or not. I could breathe into my hands and then smell it, but what if my nose was just used to my own particular bad breath odour and didn't pick up anything unusual? You get people who eat loads of raw onion for lunch, giving them breath that could floor an old person at twenty metres, but they walk around totally oblivious, even though their nose is literally five centimetres max from their mouth. I hadn't eaten any raw onion. Nor Monster Munch for that matter, but I still wasn't going to risk it, so I popped six sugar-free mints into my mouth and sucked, hoping that the potential laxative effect from the artificial sweeteners only kicked in at a much higher dose.

The bus pulled into the bus station at the edge of town and there was no time for the rest of the list. This was it. Ready or not, here I come.

I squinted as I walked in through the door at Burger Burger Burger. It hadn't struck me last time quite how bright the lights were. White. Stark. Super unflattering. Phone-light-on-the-Green-level. With Meena and Anna this would have been fine. An advantage even – oh good, I get to see my food clearly and there's no chance of feeling sleepy or accidentally leaning in some ketchup. But for a date? Even a group one? Not so much.

Typical Lisa choice. Never needing to wear 'nude' tights, opting for #nofilter on Instagram, dining in neon lighting – she flaunted her perfection at every opportunity.

I'd worried that I'd be the first one there, but the others were already cocooned in a bright red booth in the corner, food spread out in front of them. I did a lame sort of half wave and then headed to the counter to order. Cheese burger (with everything except gherkins and onions – the onions were grilled but I still wasn't taking any chances) and fries. When I got my food and approached the table, I found I was the only one with fries, as Lisa instantly and gleefully pointed out, so I pretended they were for everyone to share and then watched in resentment as Ennis and Anthony proceeded to steal most of them.

Lisa and April didn't even have buns. Just a single burger patty perched on top of a little heap of lettuce. The burger looked exposed, naked without it's doughy home. I don't get why anyone who didn't have a serious gluten intolerance would choose a bun-less burger. It's like preferring slugs to snails.

Lisa grudgingly moved seat so that I could sit next to Ennis. He greeted me with a, 'Hey babe, you look nice,' and then draped his left arm round my shoulders and we had a quick hello snog. He'd had the onions.

'Lisa's just been filling us in on her Christmas Party,' Ennis said with a wink. 'It's going to be epic. You'll come with me, won't you? It's next Saturday.' Lisa's eyes narrowed to tiny slits. Slits of some sort of super-advanced technology ray gun that bore into my skull. Ennis span round to face her and she managed a smile that ended level with the bottom of her nose. 'That's OK, isn't it Lisa, if I bring my girl.' It wasn't a question. Lisa tinkled a brittle, 'Yes, of course.'

This was it. The moment. The thing that everything had been building towards. Ennis had officially claimed me as 'his girl' and I'd just been invited to Lisa's family's Christmas Party. The most talked about event in the town social calendar. I was standing at the pinnacle of social success, planting a flag. I would be the envy of every girl in the class. In the year.

Then Ennis stood up.

'I'm getting a shake. Want one, babe? Chocolate?'

Yes. Yes I did. Ennis's babe who was accompanying him to Lisa's Christmas Party definitely wanted a chocolate shake. While he was gone, I surreptitiously texted Meena under the table.

'I'm going to Lisa's party. As Ennis's girl!'

'XXXXXXXXXX,' pinged back instantly.

Ennis returned and, smiling stupidly to myself, I started my shake.

There's a reason I don't usually have shakes.

By about halfway through I could feel the head-spinning sugar mania approaching, but I couldn't stop drinking. It was too good.

I felt too good.

Alive. Energised. Vivacious. Attractive. Plus there were no Lego men or marshmallows around so I couldn't go on some weird Patrick Swayze sugar trip. Having said that, mid-slurp my straw was blocked by an unblended bit of ice. An iceberg in a brown whirlpool. The only thing to stop the descent into the sinking sand. *Hold on Patrick, hold on.*

'Who's Patrick?' Ennis asked, looking at me weirdly.

Oh God. I thought that had all happened in my head. How much did I say out loud? He's going to think I'm a total freak.

'Um, no one,' I replied sheepishly, pushing the rest of the milkshake to the other side of the table so I wasn't tempted to drink any more.

Still, the harm had been done. I was buzzing and not coming down any time soon. I floated into World of Bowl and started gabbling on about my not being any good at bowling. About how it'd been great as a kid because you could use those inflatable tube things that blocked the gutters plus a mini slide to roll the ball in the right direction so you were pretty much guaranteed to reach the skittles at the end. Then I started on about how we should approach choosing our team name and how Meena had once entered my name as Indi-armpit and then when I'd flukily got a spare, the screen flashed up 'Congratulations Indi-armpit' for everyone there to see.

After probably ten minutes of uninterrupted blabbing, I finally registered Lisa and April's open mouths and Anthony's confused expression and shut up. Ennis was smiling at me.

'Don't I always say how funny India is?' he laughed. 'So deadpan. She cracks me up!' He turned to me and planted a still oniony kiss on my mouth. 'You know we're not actually going to bowl, right?'

'Right,' I laughed, a bit too hard. 'Course!'

Then why the hell were we here?

My attempted cover-up was about as successful as a blob of concealer atop a raised spot. Lisa openly laughed at me and explained.

'We're just sitting and loser watching. Speaking of which...'

The automatic doors slid open and in walked Rich Evans flanked by two guys who looked vaguely familiar. My heart gave an involuntary little flutter. I couldn't totally tell if it was from seeing Rich or stage one of a glucose induced heart attack.

Friday night.

Rich had said he was out with friends Friday night. I guess it wasn't that odd running into him. Friday night options were pizza at someone's house, a movie, burger or bowling. It took a few moments for me to identify the guys Rich was with. The one to his right with blond curly hair was Steve, I think, and the dark haired guy was Lee or Lucas or Luke or something. It started with an L anyway. I'd never met them properly or even spoken to them. They must have been at one of Anna's concerts. More orchestra geeks. But that's not how they appeared at the time through the sugar haze. It was like watching one of those slow motion scenes in a movie when the team of super-cool guys walk towards the camera, grimy from action, a burning building flaming away in the background.

In the back of my brain I knew that in reality it was just three slightly spotty teenage guys wearing too high waisted trousers and bad sweatshirts walking into World of Bowl, but that's what it seemed like. Honest to God. Rich and my eyes locked and a big smile spread over his face. My legs started to propel me over when Ennis's hand grabbed my arm.

'What are you doing?' he hissed.

Rich registered the arm. The Ennis. And the smile was wiped from his face. He looked at me, confused. Then angry. I'd said I was busy. I'd said I was meeting friends. It hadn't been a lie, but it hadn't really been the truth either.

And now the only boy who'd ever been really nice to me was mad.

Rich turned his back on me and headed over to the shoe desk with his mates. I willed him to turn round and look at me so I could somehow channel an apology. He didn't. They all removed their trainers and swapped them for stinky red and white leather numbers. They were bowling.

'Losers,' April whispered happily, nodding in their direction. 'This should be fun. Don't you think, India?'

I ignored her.

Rich and his friends were given the middle lane while we sat at a raised table in the 'café' section under a poster advertising grim-looking chicken wing basket deals. We didn't eat anything. I was stuffed from my burger and you know you're in trouble if the food looks that inedible in the marketing material. April and Anthony shared a Diet Coke.

At first Rich kept shooting looks in my direction. A mixture of hurt puppy and angry dog. Probably how a hurt baby pit bull would look. Either way, you wouldn't put it on a Battersea Dogs Home poster. I tried to catch his eye and communicate. But it's difficult to make your eyes look friendly, apologetic and also convey *I really like you, but kind of got pressured into this date with Ennis and really want to go to Lisa's Christmas Party.*

It didn't matter anyway. Rich soon stopped looking and started concentrating on the bowling instead. And they were having fun. Proper fun. Like a Friday night with friends should be. Part of me, basically all of me minus something small like my feet, wished I was over there instead. That I'd turned down Ennis and chosen to be with Rich.

Steve's thing was to spend ages selecting which ball to use and doing these intricate run-ups before shooting the ball super fast into the gutter and Lee/Lucas pretty consistently chipped one or two skittles off the end and then did crazy fist pumps like '2' was the best score ever. Rich had his own unique style. He'd always take a green or orange ball, like he was superstitious about it, and then, before firing it off, would furrow his brow in concentration, extend his lower lip and blow his hair off his face (turning his forehead into a skyscraper in the process). Then he'd do this tiny little bum wiggle. I think it was all subconscious but it was hilarious. Lisa and April had kept up a pretty consistent commentary throughout with Ennis and Anthony joining in now and then like sports presenters. They were nearly wetting themselves at their own incredible wit. Rich's moves were the most remarked upon. Especially by Ennis. He called them 'frickin' mint' and had this glint in his eye as he said it. For once he wasn't winking.

The Boomerang was his idea.

I didn't think he was going to go through with it. I thought it was going to be all talk like the rest of the evening. It didn't work out like that.

It was Rich's turn again. Ennis slid off his seat and walked along the back wall, looking like he was heading to the toilets. As he drew level with Rich's lane he held up his phone. Five seconds was all it took. Five seconds to capture a furrowed brow, lower lip exhale, towering forehead and bum wiggle. Playing over and over. Boomerang made it more absurd, if possible. Just the repetition of it. Like something from a Chaplin movie.

He shared it on Insta.

'You shouldn't have done that,' I said quietly as Ennis sat back down and showed us his masterpiece. It already had ninety-two likes.

'Why?' snapped April. 'Why are you so keen to protect Rich?'

Four pairs of eyes were focused on me. Piercing me.

'It's just … he seems nice, that's all.'

'Do you want to go over there and join him instead?' Lisa purred. I swear her pupils were cat eye slits.

My stomach clenched and flipped. Backing up your convictions, doing the right thing takes guts.

Lisa and April sat there, staring, sharpening imaginary knives.

I didn't do the right thing.

I sat still like the coward that I am.

India Smythe: officially gutless.

Rich and his two friends were still bowling, completely oblivious. Steve had miraculously avoided the gutter, got a strike and a big X flashed on the screen above his lane. 'Ste-inker!' I couldn't help smiling. Meena would love these guys. Rich and his other mate high-fived each other.

Rich reached into his pocket post high-five and pulled out his phone. Someone must have messaged him. Told him about the Boomerang. His mouth fell open and he looked upset. Properly upset. Then he turned towards our table. He wasn't looking at Ennis. Or Anthony. Or any of the others.

He was staring straight at me. Words were unnecessary. Turns out eyes can say quite a lot and his eyes said it all.

*How could you? How could you sit there with those people while they did that to me?*

Worst part is, he was right.

We left World of Bowl soon after Rich and his friends did. Lisa and April's enthusiasm quickly dried up when there was no one left to mock. Ennis walked me to the bus stop, but I didn't kiss him goodbye. We just sort of stood next to each other, shoulder to shoulder till my bus came.

He knew something was wrong. That I was mad. And, to give him credit, I think he felt a bit bad about it too.

'It was just a bit of fun, you know,' he ventured as the bus display counted down to two minutes. 'I'm sorry you thought it wasn't cool. And I get that. I like that about you. You make me a better person.'

I didn't say anything.

The display updated: R45 – 1 minute.

'So, I'll see you next Saturday then?'

I stayed silent.

The bus rounded the corner and I got on. Ennis stared at me as I walked down the central aisle towards an empty seat at the back. This time I didn't need to remember not to look back. I didn't want to.

I got back home just before eleven. Mum was already in bed but Dad was still up in the kitchen. He was sat at the island, halfway through assembling the drawbridge for his Lego fort. I started making myself some Marmite toast as I could feel a sugar crash coming on.

'Good night, love? You're back early.'

'It was fine.'

Dad registered my drained-looking face and the fact that I'd said 'fine'. I don't say 'fine'. Mum's the only person in the family who says 'fine' and she only says it when she's been to visit Nan and comes back with her mouth set in a thin straight line and shoulders hunched up around her ear lobes.

'Did he try anything?' Rumbles of anger appeared in Dad's voice. 'Did that boy…'

'No, Dad. Nothing like that,' I replied wearily. 'He was … mean to another boy, that's all.'

Dad's face softened. Guys being mean to other guys was apparently no biggie.

'Another boy who likes you?'

I nodded. Although 'liked' is probably more accurate now. I very much doubt Rich still has any positive feelings towards me whatsoever.

'Guys are idiots,' he said. 'They can't handle feelings. Cut him some slack, OK?' His voice dropped a few decibels. It does this when he's about to tell me something that Mum wouldn't approve of, even though Mum was asleep upstairs and couldn't possibly hear him. 'You know when I first met your mum she was actually into Kev, kind of his girl.'

No, I did not know this. This I had never been told. The official version, Dad's version anyway, has always been that they met in a bar. And Mum was wowed by Dad's crazy level of guitar skills. It was love at first sound.

'Well that night, the night we met, Kev had brought her along to the gig. I saw her and, well, I was blown away. She was smoking hot. I knew I had to have her. I cut two of Kev's guitar strings before we went on stage. Sabotaged him. My own band brother.'

Dad choked up with emotion and then managed to recover enough to keep going.

'Kev looked like an idiot, playing these really weak chords, and I had to take over his guitar solo. Stole your mum's heart with this sweet riff. So you see?'

'No.'

I was getting nothing from that story apart from understanding a bit more why Mum seems to act so weirdly around Kev.

'Good guys sometimes do bad things to get girls.'

'Right. Night, Dad.'

I was too tired for this. I went to sleep thinking about what Dad had said. Could Ennis still be a good guy? A good guy who did a bad thing? But if you do bad things doesn't that just make you bad?

Maybe I'll add Philosophy to my list of potential A-levels. Some of the stuff Chidi talks about in *The Good Place* is quite interesting.

The rest of the weekend was a bit of a write-off.

I didn't hear from Ennis till the end of Saturday, and then it wasn't a further apology it was just a, 'Hey, babe.' Meena kept texting, trying to persuade me to go outfit shopping with her, but I wasn't in the mood. Didn't even know if I wanted to go *anywhere* with Ennis again, let alone Lisa's party.

I needed something to do to take my mind off things, so on Sunday morning I ended up helping Mum prepare for the church bake sale. She isn't usually into church stuff, but would never turn down an opportunity to show off her baking skills. Plus it was a chance for her to go head-to-head with her ex-friend, Chrissie, who'd made disparaging remarks when Book Club had been disbanded in favour of Article Club.

'I'm going to knock the air out of her mousse,' Mum declared.

'She's making mousse for a bake sale?'

'No, India,' Mum snort-laughed, like I was the imbecile. 'It's a saying.'

No, Mum, it's really not.

Mum had opted for iced currant buns. 'They might seem simple, India, but I'm going for a panettone variant with two types of dough, five rises and then a double coil shape.'

I helped her knead the dough, put the water at the bottom of the oven to help the buns prove and then helped shape them. This was the most fun bit. You make a long sausage shape, smear one side with a cinnamon, sugar and currant mixture and then curl one half, one way and the other half, the other way so you end up with a conjoined twin snail shell effect. Then it was just a case of baking them for fifteen minutes, waiting for them to cool and then a bit of icing.

As a final touch, Mum asked me to halve some glacé cherries and then put a half in the centre of each swirl.

They smelt and looked delicious, but there was no time to try one – Mum had to get them to church while they were still warm, 'And show up that Prissie Chrissie.'

I wasn't going to go with her, but then she offered me a tenner to help on the stall. It was only as we were setting up that it struck me what a horrific afternoon I'd signed up for. I should have asked for way more money.

'No one else here is under fifty,' I hissed at Mum. She didn't reply, already heading off 'to check out the competition'. So I was left alone, guardian of forty iced buns priced at fifty pence each. Old people kept hobbling past, looking at the buns and sniggering. Even the ones who bought one sniggered. I didn't get it. Not until pervy old Mr Miller from the top of our street leant across the table and said, all throatily, 'Nice tits, India.'

I stared in disbelief at my top, but for once his eyes weren't resting there. They were focused downwards. At the buns. Two white circles topped with red nipples. Oh GOD!!! I was fronting a semi-erotic stall of iced breast buns.

At that exact moment, I spotted Mum, heading back my way. She wasn't alone. She had some guy next to her. Some guy my age. With curly hair. And dimples. And a massive forehead. NO, NO, NO!!!!!!!!!

Rich Evans looked at me and froze. He was clearly as surprised to see me as I was him.

'Look, India, I found another young person helping his mum out.'

'India,' Rich said stiffly.

'Rich,' I replied, equally as robot-esque.

'Oh, good. You two know each other. How much have we taken so far?'

'Eight pounds fifty,' I mumbled into the ground.

'Ha, that's fifty pence more than Chrissie. She was on eight pounds last time I checked. I knew chocolate and beetroot brownies were so 2018.'

With that, Mum sashayed off again and I was left alone with Rich against a backdrop of doughy nipples.

We stood there in silence for a few minutes as I took fifty pence pieces from more smutty old people.

Finally, I plucked up the courage to speak.

'I'm really sorry about Friday.'

'Yes, well...' he said coldly. I wasn't forgiven. I clearly wasn't forgiven. And I knew I didn't deserve to be.

'I didn't know he was going to do that.'

'People like that always do things like that.'

I didn't know what to say.

'Look, I'm going now. If you're really sorry, come to the Christmas Recital. We can talk then.'

'But...'

Rich was already walking away.

After four steps he swivelled and said, 'By the way, you do know your buns look like breasts, don't you?'

I nodded.

'I'm probably not going to Lisa's party,' I announced to Meena during first break on Monday.

'Oh, India, has Ennis dumped you? I'm so sorry!!!' she cried, giving me the nicest hug.

'No, no,' it's not like that. I don't think I want to go with him.'

She looked like she'd been hit by a stun grenade.

'Wh-wh-' She literally couldn't get the words out.

I tried to explain about Friday night, about Ennis and Rich, but Meena didn't seem outraged.

'So,' she concluded, 'as I see it, you looked overly happy to see Rich. That made Ennis, your date for the night, jealous so he reacted by doing something a bit mean. Like you're so perfect.'

When she put it like that, what Ennis had done didn't seem so totally awful. I probably *had* seemed a bit too keen to see Rich. And Ennis had felt bad about it and sort of apologised afterwards.

Then an image of Rich at the bake sale sprang to mind. He'd been cold, distant.

'But, Meena, Rich seemed really upset by it.'

'Of course he's upset. He didn't get the girl. That's life.'

Maybe she was right. She seemed so certain. And Dad had been so sure too.

'I guess.'

'So you're going?'

I took a deep breath. My mind drifted to ice sculptures and trays of profiteroles. The semi-magical event that Meena had been obsessing about for all the time I'd known her. It was my chance to see it in the flesh. Probably the only chance I'd ever get.

'OK, I'm going.'

''Course you are.'

The rest of the week sped past. It was school Literature Week and me and Anna had signed up as volunteer helpers at the start of term, so every break we were on duty helping Mrs Greenwood out in the library. We got to eat tonnes of custard creams, plus it meant I didn't have to do any more Fence visits, so there was no chance of running into Rich or having to attempt another through-the-wire-diamond snog. April and Lisa were being slightly frosty but not out and out unfriendly.

'The theme for the party is winter,' Lisa instructed on Tuesday. 'So wear something appropriate.'

Ennis texted on Wednesday to check it was OK to pick me up at six on Saturday and I texted back a cool with two Xs. I was starting to get excited. Willing Saturday to come.

Saturday came. The day started late. 10am late. I was massively confused at first – waking up to full-on sunlight. Where was the 8am maternal barge-in? The cup of tea in bed? I actually quite fancied a cup of tea in bed this morning.

'Mum?' I called softly. No answer. 'Mum?' a bit louder. Still nothing.

I padded downstairs for a cinnamon raisin bagel (and to check that the rest of my family hadn't fallen prey to the beginnings of a zombie apocalypse) and found Mum next to a mug of Nespresso. In active wear. Reassuringly normal.

'Thought I'd let you get your beauty sleep. After all … big night tonight!!!!'

Her smile was twitching like it wanted to leap off her face and samba across the kitchen island. She knew about the party. How the hell did she know about the party?!

'Ennis texted to ask permission to take you.'

*What????*

'Such a nice boy. Very chivalrous. As soon as you've had breakfast, we're going shopping for a dress. A mother-daughter day! It's going to be so much fun. Any idea about colours? I'm thinking green, to bring out your eyes. Plus holly's green so it's quite Christmassy too. What's Ennis wearing? It's best if you coordinate. Shall I text him?'

'NO!' I suddenly couldn't take it any more and just exploded at her.

I shouldn't have. She hadn't done anything wrong. Well, apart from the texting Ennis suggestion. That was off the charts horrific. But the rest of it – she was just trying to be nice. And to be fair, we didn't really do any of that stuff. Shopping, female bonding. I'm not into football or guitars or Lego, but I'm not massively into girly stuff either. Meena goes for manicures and haircuts with her mum. I hadn't realised how left out Mum felt.

'Sorry, India,' Mum replied. 'It's just it's *the* party... Rumour has it there'll be an ice sculpture!'

What is it with people and ice sculptures?!? It's basically just a slightly shinier snowman.

I had a long shower to rinse off the drowsiness and then pulled on jeans and a hoodie and headed downstairs.

'Green sounds good, Mum,' I called out as a peace offering.

'Oh, really? Oh wonderful! I'll just get some plAHstic bags and we can go.'

Mum was standing in the hall, still in her active wear.

'Are you going like that?' I asked, thinking *please no, please no, please no*.

'Oh no, of course not.' Relief washed over me. 'It's cold out. I'll just fetch my jumper.'

She returned a minute later with her waist-stopping cherry red mohair. I followed her exposed Lycra clad butt out to the car.

Mother-daughter days aren't totally awful. Mum bought me a really nice dress. Dark green, clingy but not too tight, with sequins down the front and a few strategic ruffles at chest height to give the appearance of more of a bust. It cost more than I'd normally be able to spend, but Mum said tonight was 'special'. Her level of enthusiasm was beginning to rub off on me and I was actually starting to look forward to the party later.

Dress bought, Mum announced we were going to go for a coffee.

'A coffee?' I spluttered. What about my delicate, still developing nervous system?

'Why not?' she cried, throwing caution and potential neurological damage to the wind.

There was a really cute guy behind the counter, manning the coffee machine. #nofilter cheekbones that CatrinX2000 would kill for. He smiled at me. Smiled. At me. And I adjusted my face so that my good side was facing him, before giving a goofy grin back. Mum started to order.

'I'll have a flat white, please, and my daughter will have a COFFEE TOO!' Like she was announcing breaking news. *North Korea is destroying all its nukes and India Smythe is trying coffee.*

'What sort of coffee would your daughter like?' Cute Guy replied tolerantly.

'Something weak. Not too much caffeine… How many shots are there in a babycino?'

Agggggghhhhhhhhhhhhhhhh!!!!!! If you'd X-rayed me at that precise moment you would have seen Munch's Scream.

'Babycinos are just steamed milk,' Cute Guy smirked. 'And we only serve them to under tens. Is your daughter under ten?'

My face was now the colour of Mum's jumper.

'I'll have a regular cappuccino with extra chocolate

sprinkles, please,' I squeaked, before Mum could say anything else and then stood, staring at the floor, while he steamed the milk.

I insisted we sat as far away from the counter as possible and it took ten minutes before I could speak properly again. To give Mum credit, she did actually acknowledge that she'd embarrassed me and seemed properly sorry about it. I ate the chocolately froth with a teaspoon and then sipped the coffee underneath while Mum tried to cheer me up with a steady stream of her work's juiciest gossip. At first I was like 'who cares', but towards the end I was genuinely (and slightly manically) interested to find out what was going to happen next in the saga between Sandra in Accounts and Tomas, the new German marketing intern who's fifteen years her junior but has 'a body you could crack eggs on'. I started thinking about Ennis's body. He works out a lot. His arms are really muscly. Arms you could crack eggs on. Work sounds more fun than school. Same level of drama but a loss less bitchy.

We had lunch at a deli where you perched on high stools and ate slices of overpriced cured meat and cheese and I told Mum all about the Consent Workshops and Gillian's contribution, only stopping when I saw tiny tears start to form at the edge of Mum's eyes.

'What is it?' I asked. 'I thought you'd find it funny.'

'I do. I do.' Then Mum started openly sobbing and people started looking at us and shooting me evils for being a horrid daughter who makes her mum cry.

'It's just … it's just that you shared. You shared something about school with me! I'm so happy!' And then she burst into tears all over again.

We headed home after this.

As Mum finished parking the car, she swivelled round to face me.

'India…' Her eyes did that overly wide thing they do when she's nervous.

'Do you think you might like to do something like that again sometime?'

'Yes Mum. Sure.' I think she could tell that I meant it as she had a bounce in her step as we walked up the front path.

It made her bum wobble something chronic.

Ennis rang the doorbell at six on the dot.

I was still in my room, but ready. My new green dress was on and I still liked it *and* it didn't look stupid with black tights so there were no terrible pasty, bobbly leg/natural tan tights issues. Mum had helped me blow-dry my hair so it was smooth rather than frizzy, but not too newsreader-y and my make-up was very subtle apart from some shimmery silver eye shadow that I'd managed not to smudge on the third attempt. I'd put on my black heels with the gold and silver butterfly bows to make my legs look longer and Mum had produced some gel cushion things to put in the toes to stop my feet aching later.

Dad got to the door first and my first peek at Ennis was over the banister from the top of the stairs. He looked amazing. He was wearing dark blue trousers with a matching dark blue tight-fitting jacket and a white rose in his button hole. He caught sight of me and gave me a wink and, at that moment, I thought I was the luckiest girl in the world.

Dad started being really over friendly to Ennis. Inviting him in, offering him a drink – 'Beer? – heh! – Just kidding [backslap] – or am I?' It was horrific. I'd thought it was bad when Dad hated boys. Belittling and bullying them. Turns out him liking them was even worse.

Ennis was looking really weirded out by this excessive keenness. Maybe he was worried that Dad was going to start texting him too.

'We're going,' I said, pushing Ennis towards the door. 'Night, Dad. Night, Mum.'

Mum ran into the hall.

'Take lots of photos. You can borrow my phone if you like. Or, or, I'm sure we've got a camera somewhere. Andy, where's our digital camera?'

*Andy.*

She was that excited.

'In the drawer, Sam,' Dad replied – pointing at the hall console table.

God! He was excited too!!

'I'm not taking a camera,' I said firmly.

Mum thrust it into my hand. 'Make sure you get a couple of the ice sculpture. Oh, and of Lisa's mum. I want to know what she's wearing and how she's done her hair.'

I put the camera back down on the console table and opened the door.

'Good evening, Mr and Mrs Smythe,' Ennis said formally, the perfect gentleman.

'Such lovely manners,' cooed Mum.

'Stay away from the peanuts!' called Dad.

'What?' from Ennis.

'Nothing,' I said, shutting the door, exhausted.

We walked to the end of the front path where there was an Uber already waiting. I was really conscious of the fact that I was taller than Ennis in my heels. Taller by about three centimetres. I couldn't see over the top of his head or anything, but I now know there's a mole on the top of his left ear. Ennis was clearly aware of my elevated height too as he kept shooting glances at my shoulders as if trying to work out whether it was worth even *attempting* a wrap around. It wasn't.

As we sat in the car, Ennis produced another, now slightly crumpled, white rose from his pocket.

'For you,' he said. 'May I?'

I nodded and he leant forward to pin the rose to my dress. He was staring deep into my eyes. It was an incredibly romantic moment. For all of two seconds.

'Ow!' I shrieked. The pin had gone straight through the material and into my flesh. There was a tiny dark patch on the dress from the blood.

'Oh, God, sorry, India,' he croaked.

'Don't worry, it's fine,' I replied, smile plastered on. And it was sort of OK as it didn't hurt for long and the rose, once properly in place, covered up the stain. Only the back petals turning pink.

There was a long awkward pause before Ennis turned to face me again. He was obviously thinking about last Friday. How it had ended. The whole Rich thing. I was thinking about it too and was pleased we were on the same wavelength. We hadn't talked about it. Now was the chance to clear the air.

'Forgive me?' he asked, eyes all intense through a lattice of eyelashes.

'Sure. I probably over reacted anyway. As my Dad said, sometimes good people do bad things.'

'Right.' Ennis looked unsure, confused. 'It was just an accident. The pin slipped.'

He hadn't been thinking about Rich at all. Just the rose. Only the rose.

'Sure,' I replied quietly.

Lisa's house was in the middle of a gated private estate the other end of Rainston. Ennis had to wind down the window to speak to a guard at the estate entrance to get us in. Everything about the road from the high brick walls, to the perfectly manicured front lawns to the high density of evergreen magnolias said *we're better than you. Keep out.* Even the street lamps were different. Victorian or expensive mock-Victorian, straight out of Narnia, they cast a gentle orange glow on gravel. No LEDs here. Energy efficiency had no place on South Hill Drive.

There was no mistaking which was Lisa's house. The driveway gates were open and three tall, fairy light strewn Christmas trees stood on the front lawn.

Ennis made a point of keeping me sat in the car while he walked round to my side to let me out.

He crooked his arm.

'My lady,' he said with a wink.

Everything Meena had said was right. Lisa's Christmas Party was stunning.

I felt totally out of my depth and clung to Ennis' arm as we headed in through the front door and handed our coats to someone dressed like he was out of the *Grand Budapest Hotel* movie. No one's ever taken my coat before. No one. We then weaved down a corridor, through an empty reception room with a midnight-blue, velvet sofa in the corner, so spotless that no one could have ever sat on it, into another room that had no discernible purpose and then out of some French windows into the back garden.

We passed waiters in starched white collars and black waistcoats carrying trays of Kir Royal (champagne and blackcurrant cordial, as Ennis explained to me) and platters of smoked salmon blinis and mini venison burgers and towering pyramids of profiteroles. I sort of wished I had brought Mum's camera.

One of the waiters paused in front of me, platter outstretched.

'Ma'am?'

'Um … yes please!' I took one of each and Ennis laughed at me as I tried not to drop the venison burger while tucking into the blini. Delicious. Totally delicious.

Plus the venison burger came in a bun. I wanted to go back for a profiterole but Ennis tugged me forward.

'They won't run out,' he laughed at me, genuinely surprised. I don't think he'd ever seen a girl eat before.

Lisa was holding court with her parents on the back terrace. She looked amazing, I have to give her that. Blond hair long and loose, legs bare, tight silver dress and matching heels. If winter had wanted to be personified and look good it would have chosen to appear as Lisa Hartley that night. Lisa's mum was basically an older version of Lisa. Hair up in a sort of loosish, swept-up style; white, pencil-skirted dress (I made a mental note for Mum) – she was elegant and even seemed natural. Her plastic surgeon must be the best of the best.

'Let's go and say hi,' Ennis suggested and started to walk over. Because I was surgically attached to his arm, I had to go too.

'Hi, babe,' Lisa purred to Ennis. She gave me a sideways glance that then travelled up and down. 'India … green? How… festive.' Before I had a chance to be hurt, we were ambushed from behind.

'Ennis!' April wrapped her arms round Ennis in an inappropriately intimate hug. Anthony was with her and he and Ennis did some weird macho backslap, hand bump rubbish.

'So pleased you're here,' April smiled. At Ennis. Then she turned to me. 'I love your dress.' I couldn't help it. A big smile leapt onto my face. April Jones loved my dress.

'It's so … Santa's little helper.' Tinkle laugh.

Ha. Ha. Ha.

I registered April's dress: silvery-white lace.

I looked around the garden. All the girls were in shades of silver and white. A scattering of diamonds against the night sky. Suddenly my dress no longer seemed so glamorous. The ruffles looked tacky. The black tights desperate.

April was right. I was the Christmas elf to their snow queens.

'Excuse me a minute.' I had to get away. Be anywhere but there.

'I'll come with you, Babe.' Ennis treated the others to a quick, 'Laterz,' and then caught me up.

'Inside or outside?' he said, head angled slightly and eyelashes batting.

'Outside,' I replied. I needed air. Needed to breathe. We headed down the lawn, which was lined with heaters and clusters of people standing and talking.

In the bottom right corner was a jazz band. They were really good. Even totally non-musical me could tell that. The singer's voice was soft and husky and hypnotic and she was jaw-droppingly beautiful. Like God had lost count when he was handing out good qualities and she'd got a double dose.

We stopped to listen and Ennis wrapped his arms round my waist. I tried not to focus on his above-ear mole.

'Let's dance,' I murmured to Ennis. I could no longer see Lisa and April, the lights were twinkling in the trees and the singer was crooning about love. I wanted to dance with my guy.

'Yeah!' laughed Ennis. 'Let's.' His feet didn't move. A couple of seconds more and a frown crossed his face as he suddenly realised I was serious. 'Nah, this isn't a dancing party. People don't dance.'

There was an awkward pause.

'Are you having a good time?' he asked.

'Yes,' I lied. 'It's just I'm not sure I fit in. Look at the other girls here. They're all silver and sparkly. They're diamonds.'

'So?' Ennis stared straight into my eyes. Well, straight and up a little bit, and he hit me with full wattage intensity. 'Maybe I prefer emeralds.'

It was the best line. All my doubts about him evaporated on the spot. I smiled back, matching him watt for watt.

'So, do you want to go upstairs?' he asked.

I shook my head. I wasn't ready for this. I hadn't

wanted to lie down behind the benches with Yan on the Green and I didn't want to go upstairs now with Ennis.

'Oh … OK … later.' Ennis sounded annoyed now and his eyes dimmed. 'Let's check out the ice sculpture.' Ennis gestured towards the centre of the lawn. There it was: the pièce de résistance. The ice sculpture. A ring of people surrounded it like a halo.

I'd never seen an ice sculpture before and now I kind of got what all the fuss what about. It was beautiful. A young girl, caught mid-dance with hands outstretched, her dress twirling round her legs. What's more, it was connected up to some sort of internal fountain so that icy water seemed to spring from her palms and then cascade to the floor into this pool. Jets of icy air were blown at it from three sides to prevent it melting. The air was filled with 'Oohhh's and 'Aahhhh's.

We stood and stared at it, not talking.

'Ennis, you're needed!' Lisa's voice trilled from the side of the lawn. 'India, can we steal him for a moment?'

Ennis clearly wanted to go, so I nodded my OK and he bounded off, a bit too enthusiastically.

What now? I had to move. To circulate. I couldn't be the weirdo who just stared at the ice sculpture all evening.

I moved back towards the side of the lawn and

hovered. How to look busy? To look like I was popular and circulating and confident?

A train of waiters kept passing by so I decided just to eat. It would give me something to do with my hands, an excuse not to be talking.

I hoovered up profiterole after profiterole. They were delicious – soft, creamy, with the finest dark chocolate on top. Mum would have approved.

One of the waiters, a younger one, probably eighteen or nineteen and really hot, kept shooting me glances as he passed and I smiled back each time. This was excellent. Maybe when Ennis came back he'd see the hot waiter hitting on me and feel really jealous. *Come over, come over*, I internally chanted and on the third walk-by he did. The hot waiter actually came over and stopped right in front of me.

'I'm sorry,' he said, very seriously (the poor boy was clearly nervous), 'I have to tell you…'

'I'm sorry,' I cut him off, 'but I have to tell *you* – I have a boyfriend.' Stopping him for his own sake before he confessed undying love. Direct was best. He wanted me, I was attracted to him too, but I had a boyfriend.

'No … what? It's just that you have a blob of cream on your chin.'

'Oh … thank you.'

Earth swallow me now.

He handed me a napkin and then disappeared.

No one offered me any more profiteroles.

I looked to see where Ennis had gone, but couldn't see him through the throng of people. The chances of spotting him were diminishing too. The garden was getting fuller and fuller and all the girls were wearing heels.

Scanning the sea of faces, I finally spotted one which I recognised. I had to do a double take as it was so unexpected. But there was no mistaking a certain very distinctive monobrow.

'Gillian!' I called, enthusiastically. 'Gillian, it's me – India!'

She seemed a bit taken aback by my excitement, but at least stayed still so I had a new place to stand. A refuge. A refuge clad in a bright scarlet dress. The berry to my holly.

'I'm surprised to see you here,' I blurted out before I realised how it was going to sound.

'Yeah. Not sure why I am,' Gillian replied, completely unoffended. 'It's not really my scene. I thought she'd invited the whole year group.'

'Right. No...'

There was a pause, but it wasn't too awkward.

'I like your dress,' Gillian offered.

'Thanks.'

'It's like dark AstroTurf.'

It was a weird compliment, but with its own poetry.

'Do you think there'll be any games later?' Gillian asked hopefully. I could see the image of a ball bounce across her thoughts.

'Hmm. Doubt it.'

'Yeah, me too.'

Then Gillian excused herself to go to the loo and I was alone again, left to feign an interest in the leafless plants growing in the flowerbed behind.

A pair of hands sneaked round my waist and someone kissed the back of my neck.

I span round.

'It's taken me ages to find you, babe,' Ennis purred throatily. 'Where've you been?'

'I came to see the sculpture, then ended up talking to Gillian.'

'Gillian?' He laughed as if this was the funniest thing ever and then got his face under control again. 'Sorry about that babe. Didn't mean for you to be left with the stooge.'

'What? I don't get it. And why is Gillian even here?'

'It's a thing we do.' Ennis started cracking up again. 'Every party we invite a stooge.'

'You're not being any clearer.' That wasn't quite true. I think I got it. I was pretty sure I got it. I just needed him to confirm.

'A stooge. A loser. Throw them into the mix and see what happens. It's hilarious.'

'So Gillian's the stooge.'

'Exactly!'

My mind rewound to Anthony's party. Rich hiding out in the garden. Rich saying 'I'm not sure why they invited me'.

'And at Anthony's party, Rich was the stooge.'

'You got it. Genius, isn't it?!'

'And what exactly do you do to the stooge?' My voice was now ice shavings, but Ennis didn't seem to get it. Looking back on our time together, he didn't seem to get very much.

'Nothing.' He looked confused. 'Just watch them squirm. Maybe film it. We don't *do* anything.'

And that was it. It was like Ennis had just summarised his life. Their lives. *We don't do anything.*

The scales finally fell from my eyes and I could see properly. See Ennis for

what he was. See them all for what they were. Dad was wrong. Ennis wasn't a good person who'd done a bad thing. He was a bad person. Who did bad things, but mainly did nothing at all. They all were. Are. From the outside they were all sparkly and beautiful. Diamonds. Highly prized and valued. But we did diamond in Chemistry last week and, at its heart, diamond is just an allotrope of carbon. Carbon atoms arranged so that they're bonded to four other carbon atoms. Bonded to three other carbon atoms and they'd be graphite. Pencil lead. Lisa, April, Anthony, Ennis – all held in such high esteem, but they were basically pencil lead. Erasable. Why was I wasting my life with erasable people?

'I'm going,' I said sharply.

'What?' Ennis looked visibly shaken. Girls clearly didn't walk out on him very often. 'Where? I thought we could go upstairs, you know?' His voice sounded desperate now. Small and desperate and pathetic.

'There's somewhere else I'd rather be.'

'Oh. Right.'

'*Laterz*, Ennis.'

Much, much laterz.

I found Gillian heading back into the garden from the loo and caught her arm.

'You're coming with me.'

I explained about the party, about why she was there. I tried to break it nicely, but there wasn't that much sugar coating that could be done.

'Thanks, India,' she said tightly. 'I didn't think you'd liked me since Year 7 so it's good of you to tell me.'

'Sorry about that,' I replied. 'I've been such an idiot.'

'No,' she replied. 'It's fine. We've nothing in common anyway.'

'Right,' I replied with new respect. This was awesome. Direct communication where everyone understands each other and no one gets hurt. Gillian was the most underrated, coolest person ever.

'So let's get out of here,' I added.

A vein in Gillian's forehead was pumping, sending her monobrow into wave formation. A caterpillar, crossing.

'Not quite yet,' she replied. 'There's something I need to do first.'

'What?' I asked, suddenly anxious. I should have waited till we were out of here to tell her, I thought. I should have waited till we were far, far away. Ennis, Lisa and Co deserved everything they got, but I didn't think it would be a great idea for Gillian to go all Karate Kid on them.

'Don't kick anyone,' I warned.

'This doesn't call for a dick-kicking,' she replied seriously. 'This calls for something petty and bitchy and devious like the low lives they are. You stand out less. You're not the joke here. Fetch a bottle of blackcurrant cordial and meet me by the fountain.' There was something about the way she spoke that made me obey unquestioningly. I get why Gillian is always captain of the sports team.

I sneaked into the kitchen. It was a hive of activity. Waiters refilling platters, cooks piping cream into profiteroles.

One of the waiters, thankfully not cream-on-chin guy, caught me trying to weasel in. I'd get a pretty low Top Trumps stealth rating.

'Can I help you?' he asked, his accent as cut-glass as the champagne flutes.

'Um … I need a bottle of cordial, please,' I squeaked, my voice suddenly that of a pre-pubescent boy.

He raised an eyebrow but asked no further questions.

'Certainly.'

He returned, carrying a bottle.

Cradling the cordial, I scuttled out the back door and over to the fountain.

The ring of admirers had thinned; there were just five or so, all standing round the front, admiring the detail of the girl's face. Gillian was waiting and she signalled me round to the back, so that we were screened from the house and the terrace.

'It's a sealed circuit pump system,' she whispered. 'I

noticed it earlier. The same water is circulated round and round.'

Without another word of explanation, Gillian took the cordial and emptied the bottle into the base of the pool, next to the pump, then grabbed my hand and walked away.

There were about three or four more 'Ooh's and 'Aahhh's before the 'Aggghhhhhhh!!!!'s started.

'Keep walking,' hissed Gillian.

But I couldn't resist one glance back. And it was worth it. The whole evening was worth it. Plumes of red were spurting from the ice girl's hands. It was a horror show. Ice girl had just slit her wrists.

In movies and on TV, if someone decides they want to leave a party and head elsewhere to try and get the guy, they jump in a car and zoom off to the soundtrack of squealing tyres and uplifting 80s music. Something like *One Way or Another* by Blondie would have been appropriate.

Real life doesn't work like that. At least not when you're fourteen, you can't drive and, if you're me, you don't even have a phone with a taxi app, with any apps.

In real life, you walk back down the length of the private estate, freezing now that you're away from the outside heaters, your feet killing in heels despite the gel pads and then wait twenty-seven minutes for the R23 to show up.

'Heading home?' Gillian asked as we waited. I think it was to kill time rather than out of any genuine interest.

'No. St Joseph's,' I replied. 'Christmas Recital.'

'Oh?' Gillian seemed actually interested now. 'I didn't think you were an orchestra type. You're really bad at music. Is Anna playing?'

'Yes, but … it's not Anna I'm going to see.'

'Let me guess … a guy.' Gillian rolled her eyes like I was the most boring, predictable person ever.

'Yes, actually,' I replied, a bit huffily. 'A really nice guy – Rich Evans. He's into me. Or was. And I'm pretty into him too, I've just been a bit of a moron about it.'

Gillian was only half listening, but she suddenly snapped back to attention.

'Rich Evans?' she repeated.

'Yup.'

'Oh, he's lovely. He once threw a football back over the fence for me. You should have said. What time does the recital start?'

'Hours ago.' I checked my watch. It was now 9:12pm. 'Rich is going on last. Around ten-ish.'

'You'll never make it,' Gillian stated. 'It'll take fifteen

minutes into Rainston, then you have to change bus there. If you factor in the next journey plus waiting time, we're talking an hour at least.'

My heart sank. I was going to miss the Recital. I wasn't going to be able to make things good with Rich. I was going to be a social pariah. Life was bad.

Totally bad.

Gillian must have noticed my sunken face as she sprang into action and took over.

'Don't worry,' she declared. 'I'll make it work. There's a favour I can call in. A girl in Year 13, Molly. Nice girl, weak name. She drives. I'll get her to take us.'

'Us?'

'I'm not going to miss this.'

Miraculously, Molly answered her phone. I could only half hear her end of the conversation, but there was something to do with Gillian taking over organising a hockey tournament. In any event, the result was all that mattered.

Ten minutes later and Molly pulled up at the bus stop in a battered, blue Ford Fiesta. Me and Gillian jumped in. There were no squealing tyres, Taylor Swift rather than Blondie was on the radio and Molly stayed resolutely below the speed limit and obeyed a very intense mirror-signal-manoeuvre approach to driving. None of this mattered, it was all still pretty epic.

There was no problem finding the Recital. As Molly pulled into the car park in front of St Joseph's, we could already hear the muffled notes and slight screeches of a rendition of *Defying Gravity* coming from the open windows of the hall.

'Is that him?' Gillian asked.

I shook my head. I'm pretty sure that no one with balls could hit those top notes. It had to be Clara Bennett in Year 12. Anna said she was always going on about how if they'd filmed *Glee* in the UK, then she'd definitely have been cast as Rachel. Listening to the school windows threatening to crack, I can say she definitely wouldn't have been.

'Come on then! We still have time!' Gillian grabbed my hand and started sprinting towards the entrance.

I tripped and face planted in my heels.

Heels.

I'd never make it at this rate. Swept up in the drama, I kicked them off, abandoning them by a 'Don't Walk on the Grass' sign, and chased, shoeless, after her.

We reached the door to the hall as the song was ending. Gillian flung open the door, which hit the wall with a bang, and I tumbled in after her. A hundred pairs of eyes swivelled round to discover the source of the commotion and the music petered out. Mrs Trent, who was standing at the back, shhh-ing people, stared in fury; laser gunning us with her eyes.

'India, Gillian, this is quite the surprise. Quite the entrance.'

She took one look at me, my cheeks red from running, pieces of grass peeking out from the bottom of my black tights.

'I'm not even going to ask. Take a seat, quietly, and no more interruptions. We'll talk about this on Monday.'

People were still staring as we sheepishly crept down the rows, looking for an empty chair.

A frantically waving arm helped me identify Anna, sat in the first few rows reserved for performers. She looked beyond thrilled to see me there, so that at least was good. Up on the stage, at the edge, clutching his cello and waiting to go on next, was Rich. I tried to catch his eye and sent him a manic smile. I'm not sure if he saw me, but I got nothing in return.

'Miss! Miss!' A call from the stage. Clara.

'Yes?' Mrs Trent's voice could have reversed global warming.

'I didn't get to finish, so can I start again?'

A collective groan went up round the hall.

'No, Clara, I think that was more than enough, thank you.'

The hall breathed a sigh of relief.

Mr Hopper, St Joseph's music teacher, leapt onto stage to block a potential unrequested encore, and moved onto his next introduction.

'Well, that brings us onto our final act of the evening, a very talented singer and cellist, Rich Evans. And he's got a special treat for us tonight! I'll leave the rest to him.'

There was a burst of applause and Rich stepped to the middle of the stage where the microphone was.

'Hi, um ... everyone. Tonight, I wanted to try something a bit different.' He was so nervous. His cheeks were reddening and my heart went out to him.

'I thought, to end the night, I'd try a bit of audience participation and invite a member of the audience up to duet with me. So somebody ... come on up!' He did this practised arm flourish that must have looked better in his bathroom mirror than it did on stage or he never would have pulled it.

There was silence. No movement. Nothing.

Then chairs started to creak. People started to whisper.

*Go up, someone, go up*, I willed the audience.

Clara stood up, but Mrs Trent told her to sit down again. She'd had her turn.

Rich's cheeks were getting redder. He was looking

super stressed. He extended his bottom lip and exhaled, sending his hair up in a quiff and lengthening his forehead. I heard someone mutter, 'bum wiggle' and a titter of laughter ran around the room.

No one was showing any signs of going up; little whispers of ridicule spreading throughout the room like a viral video.

This was wrong. This was so unfair. This nice, kind, good guy wasn't going to just stand there and get mocked. Get laughed at in part because of what some stupid, ignorant idiot I'd kind of being going out with had done.

Tonight was meant to be about putting an end to that.

Tonight was meant to be about standing up.

No one else was going to do it.

So I stood up.

A hundred pairs of eyes swivelled to look at me for the second time that evening. My legs started to shake and every fibre of my being wanted to sit down again.

'Do I have a volunteer, then?' Rich had his hand above his eyes trying to see past the lights.

'Don't you dare chicken out now,' hissed Gillian.

'Um... Yes!' I replied.

I began the agonising walk up to the stage. It was that time in assembly all over again, but this time the lamb was willingly sacrificing itself. And as I got to the front, Rich realised for the first time who his volunteer was, and his eyes glowed with an intensity that matched his cheeks.

I climbed up the steps onto the stage, trying to focus on Rich's face rather than the two hundred people looking at me, then shuffled over so that I was stood next to him. Well, not quite stood. More crouched. By now Rich was seated, cello between his legs, microphone at his face height. I had to do a weird half squat so that my face was level with his.

'Ladies and Gentlemen, tonight we'll be singing *I Wan'na Be Like You.*' Singing. Hearing the word out loud made my insides flip. *Singing!!!*

Rich turned to me. 'Do you know the lyrics?'

'Sort of,' I replied, trying to hold back my impending coronary. 'I could do the *doo-be-doo* bits?' I offered.

'It's a deal.' And then he smiled. A lovely genuine, crinkly eye, wrinkly forehead grin without a wink in sight.

Rich started to play and somehow he made the cello sound cool. He mainly plucked rather than bowed it to give it a bit of a double bass, jazzy sound, and his voice was clear and deep, and not a bit nervous. He had to kick me to come in with a 'doo-be-doo', which I thought sounded OK, but caused a hundred people to wince in unison. Rich's voice started to waver and I felt awful. I was ruining his song. Ruining his night with my terrible, terrible singing. But then I looked closer, properly at his face, and saw that he was laughing. Every time we hit a chorus and I had to *doo-be-doo*, chairs creaked as audience members squirmed and little tears formed at the corner of Rich's eyes and started spilling down his cheeks. It should have been mortifying, this public self-shaming, but somehow it wasn't. It was OK. It was pretty funny.

We got to the end of the song and stood up to a tiny smatter of lackluster applause interspersed with some loud whoops from Anna and Gillian before slinking off to the wings.

Backstage, the lights were low and my eyes took a few seconds to adjust to the darkness. I was standing there with Rich, surrounded by black curtains, and it felt like we were in our own private universe. Like I had him completely to myself.

'Thanks,' he said, a broad grin on his face. 'Thanks for doing that for me.'

'It's OK,' I replied, trying to stop grinning and failing.

'You know you're the worst singer I've ever heard?' he added.

'Worse than Clara Bennett?'

'Even worse than Clara Bennett.'

I hid my face in my hands in a combination of laughter and embarrassment. But when I looked up, Rich had gone all serious and I realised my face mirrored his.

It was apology time.

'Rich… I'm sorry. I don't know how else to say it. You were right. Ennis … he's a bad person. And I … I was unforgivably weak and mean just letting him do stuff.'

'It's OK.' Rich's face was unreadable. 'You're free to date who you want.'

'But I don't want to. Not any more. Not Ennis, anyway.'

'Really?'

'Really.'

The air crackled.

'But you're not against dating per se?'

'No, not at all,' I replied, my voice heavy with implication. 'Not with the right guy.'

Rich nodded, almost not daring to take on what I was saying.

'And … do you have any idea who the right guy might be?'

'A pretty good idea.'

And then I shot him a massive grin and he grinned right back at me.

'Well…' he hesitated. 'I guess… I guess I should probably do this then…' and he bent his head down and kissed me. His lips were soft, our teeth didn't clash and he hadn't had the onions. It was perfect.

He broke away and just looked at me.

'Was that OK?'

I nodded happily and stared back at him. His smiling mouth, his dimples, his crinkly eyes, his curly hair. Even his forehead looked good. No longer ridiculously high, but manly, majestic.

The sort of forehead you could crack eggs on.

It was a moment later that the spell was broken. Ripped apart. By a squealing male soprano voice coming from halfway down the hall.

'India Smythe? Has anyone seen India Smythe?' came the choirboy tones. 'She wasn't at the party where she was meant to be. One of her friends said she might be here.'

No, No, NO!!!!

I peeked round the curtain.

Dad.

This couldn't get any worse.

'Andrew, she's definitely here. I found her shoes on the grass.'

Mum.

Complete with leggings and non-butt covering jumper.

I had to deal with this. Like a plaster. Rip it off. Get it over with.

'I'm here,' I hissed, emerging from the wings, Rich squeezing my hand for support.

'India, thank God, we...' And then Dad stopped. Looking Rich up and down, a light bulb going off in his head.

'What ... what...' he spluttered, purple faced. 'What are you doing here with that ... pervert?'

They dragged me away across the hall through the crowds of people filing out. But I looked back, and Rich was smiling. Clearly mortified, but smiling.

I smiled back.

And so ends another day in the Smythe household.

A glorious, wonderful day.

# ACKNOWLEDGMENTS

Huge thanks to my husband for his constant encouragement and support. Thanks to Nina and Vicky for their invaluable feedback on early drafts. Thanks to my agent, Jane Turnbull, for her fire and drive. Thanks to Earl, my incredible editor. Thanks to Nina Duckworth for her fantastic cover illustration and to Anne Glenn for the overall cover design – I love it! Thanks to all my teen readers and reviewers and to the amazing librarians who helped connect us, including Lucy Atherton, Edward Benton, Tracy Briggs, Helen Cleaves, Deirdre Gannon, Davina Jones, Tony Jones, Irene Marillat, Lucas Maxwell, Angela Platt, Jane Richardson and Sam Young. Thanks to Kirsty Ridge for her eagle-eyed proof reading. And finally, thanks to my parents.

**Sarah Govett** graduated with a First in Law from Trinity College, Oxford. After qualifying as a solicitor she set up her own tutoring agency before turning her energies to writing. Her first trilogy, *The Territory*, won the Trinity Schools Book Award and the Gateshead Teen Book Award and was described by the *Guardian* Children's Books site as 'the 1984 of our time'.

Sarah is an in-demand speaker at secondary schools and has appeared at the Southbank Literature Festival, the Edinburgh International Book Festival, the Bradford Literature Festival and the Godolphin Literature Festival.

She lives in London with her husband and three young children.

Want to be the first to hear about the further
adventures of India Smythe?

Join the mailing list:
www.sarahgovett.com
Or follow me on instagram/twitter @sarahgovett

# THE TERRITORY
# (a dystopian trilogy)

Noa Blake is just another normal 15 year old with exams looming. Except in The Territory normal isn't normal. The richest children have a node on the back of their necks and can download information, bypassing the need to study.

In a flooded world of dwindling resources, Noa and the other 'Norms' have their work cut out even to compete. And competing is everything – because everyone who fails the exams will be shipped off to the Wetlands, which means a life of misery, if not certain death.

But how to focus when your heart is being torn in two directions at once?

Winner of the TSBA 2018
'The 1984 of our time' the *Guardian* children's books
'A truly exceptional novel' *Booktrust*
'Thrilling and thought-provoking' *The Times*
'Gripping dystopia with a keen political edge' Imogen
Russell Williams, *Metro*